By: International Bestselling Author
Sapphire Knight

Sapphire Knight

Daydream
Copyright © 2017 by Sapphire Knight

Cover Design by CT Cover Creations
Editing by Mitzi Carroll
Formatting by Formatting Done Wright

This book is a work of fiction. The names, characters, places, and incidents are products of the writer's imagination or have been used fictitiously and are not to be construed as real. Any resemblance to persons, living or dead, actual events, locales or organizations is entirely coincidental.

Also by Sapphire:

Oath Keepers MC Series

Secrets
Exposed
Relinquish
Forsaken Control
Friction
Princess
Sweet Surrender – free short story
Daydream

Russkaya Mafiya Series

Secrets
Corrupted
Unwanted Sacrifices
Undercover Intentions
Russian Roulette

Standalones

Gangster
Unexpected Forfeit
1st Time Love

WARNING

This novel includes graphic language and adult situations. It may be offensive to some readers and includes situations that may be hotspots for certain individuals. This book is intended for ages 18 and older due to some steamy spots. This work is fictional. The story is meant to entertain the reader and may not always be completely accurate. Any reproduction of these works without Author Sapphire Knight's written consent is pirating and will be punished to the fullest extent of the law.

ACKNOWLEDGEMENTS

My husband - I love you more than words can express. Thank you for the support you've shown me. Some days you drive me crazy, other days I just want to kiss your face off. Who knew this would turn out to be our life, but in this journey, I wouldn't want to spend it with anyone else. Thanks for falling for my brand of crazy. I love you, I'm thankful for you, I can't say it enough.

My boys - You are my whole world. I love you both. This never changes, and you better not be reading these books until you're thirty and tell yourself your momma did not write them! I can never express how grateful I am for your support. You are quick to tell me that my career makes you proud, that I make you proud. As far as mom wins go; that one takes the cake. I love you with every beat of my heart and I will forever.

My Beta Babes - Wendi Stacilaucki-Hunsicker, Tamra Simons, Sarah Free, Jamie Weber, Lindsay Lupher and Patti Novia West. Thank you for all the love you've shown me over the past few years. You've each helped me grow in different ways throughout this entire experience and I'm forever grateful. This wouldn't be possible without you. I can't express my gratitude enough for each of you. I say I have a new book and you drop what you're doing to help me out. How did I get so lucky to have your friendship and support?

We each have other stuff going on in our lives and yet you still figure out how to make time for me, thank you so much!

My friend aka adopted mom aka sista from anotha mista - Patti Novia West, you made my year coming to Chicago. I can't thank you enough, your support is amazing, and I will never forget it. Thank you for giving me your friendship, I will value it always. You have a special place in my heart, and I can't wait to see you again. I love you, woman!

My sweet friend - Lindsay Lupher, thank you for continuing to show me so much support on this crazy journey. I've been able to count on you since day one, and that really means so much to me. I'm lucky to have you!

Editor Mitzi Carroll – You're one of the most dedicated, kindest people I've come across in this industry. I will forever be grateful that J.C. Valentine suggested I ask for your help. I was lost at a time in my career, and you literally jumped in and saved me. I will never forget that or how much you've helped me grow since then. You are a true gem, and I look forward to finally getting to hug you in Cincinnati! Your hard work makes mine stand out, and I'm so grateful! Thank you for pouring tons of hours into my passion and being so wonderful to me.

Cover Designer CT Cover Creations – You blow me away with each design! I don't know how you do it, but you make me speechless over and over. I cannot thank you enough for the wonderful work you've done for me and the amazing friendship you've offered. Your support truly means so much!

Photographer Wander Aguiar and team - Thank you so much for the amazing support you've been kind enough to show me. I look forward to future collaborations and fun times.

Model Jonny James – Thank you for being such a great person to work with and a good sport about being 'a biker guy.' You capture my character beautifully.

Formatter Brenda Wright – Thank you for making my work look professional and beautiful. I truly appreciate it and the kindness you've shown me. I look forward to working with you many times in the future and hopefully one day tasting one of those delicious cupcakes you're always posting photos of!

My Blogger Friends –YOU ARE AMAZING! I LOVE YOU! No really, I do!!! You take a new chance on me with each book and in return share my passion with the world. You never truly get enough credit, and I'm forever grateful!

My Readers – I love you. You make my life possible, thank you. I can't wait to meet many of you this year and in the future!

Sapphire Knight

COMMON MC TERMS

MC - Motorcycle Club

Prez - President

VP - Vice President

SAA - Sgt. at Arms

Ol' Lady - Significant Other

Chapel - Place Where Church is Held

Clubhouse/ Compound – MC home base

Church - MC 'Meeting'

Oath Keepers/Widow Makers hybrid charter:

Viking – Prez,

Was the heir to the Widow Makers MC,

Previous NOMAD

Blaze – Acting VP,

Previously a Widow Maker and Vikings Cousin

Torch – SAA,

Previously a Widow Maker, grew up with Viking

Scot – Oldest member,

Used to be in charge of the NOMADS

Bronx – Newest patched member,

Was prospect for the Widow Makers MC

Chaos – Usually out handling business with the

NOMADS,

Ex NFL football player

Nightmare – Close friend to Viking and Exterminator,

Previous NOMAD

Saint and Sinner – Hell Raisers,

Previous NOMADS

Smokey – Treasurer

Previously a Widow Maker

Odin – Future VP, Vikings younger brother,

Previously a Widow Maker

NOMADS:

Exterminator

Ruger

Spider

Original Oath Keepers MC:

Ares - Prez

Daydream

Cain – VP

2 Piece – Gun Runner - SAA

Twist – Unholy One

Spin – Treasurer

Snake –

Newest patched member, previous President's son

Capone – Deceased

Smiles – Deceased

Shooter – Deceased

Scratch – Deceased

Sapphire Knight

DEDICATION

I don't even know who this one should be dedicated to honestly. I think I'm going to say this one is for me. I missed my bikers like crazy, and Daydream poured from my fingertips in a matter of weeks. That's never happened to me so quickly before, and I'm over the moon, completely grateful and proud of myself.

I reached a new personal goal that I didn't realize I had tucked away inside. After publishing so many books it's easy to lose focus of the little things; writing Daydream brought that focus back.

So whoever helped motivate and inspire me, thank you.

This one is for me, for you, for all of us.

Sapphire Knight

PROLOGUE

NIGHTMARE

15 Years Old...

She's crying again. I hate it when they cry, makes me feel sick inside. My stomach churns as her hands cover her face and my father rolls his eyes at her. He hurt her; he hurts them all. They treat him like a king, and he breaks them. *Every. Single. One.*

"Come on, Dad, let's finish." I try to distract him.

"We are son. Had to teach the stupid bitch a lesson."

Her shoulders shake as her silent weeps rack her thin body. He's a bastard, and I hate him for it. He's the only person I have in my life, so in same aspect, I love him. He's my father—abusive drunk or not. This one makes wife number four. They're always young and beautiful and so, so dumb for believing his lies.

"I can't believe we're almost done." I splash some gasoline over the rebuilt carburetor so he can try and crank it over.

"This old beast will be good as new. Hell, even better—just you watch, boy. Nothing like a three-fifty small block in a Chevy like this. She'll blow any motherfucker away who tries to come up next to us." He cackles and climbs behind the wheel, taking a large sip of his beer as he slides onto the seat.

I push the piece of metal a few times that my dad pointed out last time. It pumps gasoline into the system without flooding it if you do it the right amount of times.

"Here goes!" he shouts out the open door. I poke my head around the hood and give him a thumbs-up.

The starter turns over, the fan whirring as the powerful, small block screams to life. The three-inch straight pipe running off the newly-installed headers makes the oversized piece of metal sound like one powerful beast of a machine just like my father said it would.

It roars loudly as my dad gives it a hefty pump of gas and my chest bursts with pride. *I helped do this.* My father and I actually did something together from start to finish.

He waves his hand out the window, gesturing me over. "I want you to drive it. You helped, so you earned it."

"No, Dad, you first."

"Chickenshit, boy?" He loves to give me a hard time, wants me to think I'm weak, but inside I'm not. I'm one person he can't break; my walls are too accustomed to his angry words when he's piss drunk.

"No, sir; I want to watch you and then take my turn."

"Well, load up, and we'll go fuck with old man Percy up there glaring down at us from his porch. Stupid bastard!" he hoots, pretty lit from the twelve pack he's already killed today.

No doubt he'll be taking the truck to town for more beer as well. I don't want to be along for that ride. It's not even four p.m., and he's downed twelve beers. I don't know how he can walk, let alone function like he does. It's normal though, he's this way a lot. When he's sober—which is rare—he's almost normal. It sucks, but this is life.

"I need to watch to make sure there's no smoke from anything."

"Good thinking." He nods, buying my excuse.

I know not to argue with him; he can flip a switch from happy to angry in a flash. I don't know what makes me come up with the excuses this time, but something pushes them out of me, telling me not to ride along.

He casts a mischievous grin my way, turning up "Welcome to the Jungle" by Guns and Roses as he slams the door closed and throws the truck into gear. The music pours out the open windows as he guzzles the rest of his beer. The exhaust competes with the speakers, eventually winning out as he romps on it to spin the tires.

The now-empty can he had goes flying into the yard, and then he's off. Tearing up the street toward the neighbor's house.

Percy Dickson hates us; he's always hated us. My dad says it started back when he was in middle school, and Percy was in high school. My dad supposedly kicked Percy's ass in front of a group of people, but I don't know if it's true. Dad says he was being bullied and stood up for himself. I doubt that's really what happened though. My dad always likes to start trouble. He's been in the back of a cop car too many times to count.

It takes mere moments before my father's driving in Percy's front yard, steering the big blue Chevy truck in circles. He does donuts over and over, chewing up the neighbor's grass. The ground's still a bit soft from the rain we had yesterday, so dirt and bright green turf fly off the tires in every direction.

The angry neighbor stands on his porch, waving his hands, screaming something, and I shake my head at the scene. I know my dad's loving every minute of it. This isn't the first time he's done something like this either.

"You should go clean yourself up while he's busy," I suggest to wife number four and nod toward the small house. My dad built it with his own two hands. It's not much, but he never lets us forget that he created it and he can take it away.

Besides being a mechanic and a drunk, my dad's one hell of a builder. His skills in masonry are something men around here admire. If only he could stay sober long enough to be successful with it. No one admires his inability to finish products or stay professional.

I watch the woman curled up on the floor, as she wipes her tears away and tries to pull herself together enough to get in the house. If he comes back and sees her like this, he'll get even angrier, and no matter how badly I feel, I can't ever save them from him. He's too strong. I can only sit back and hope she smartens up soon to get away from him before he does some serious damage.

A shot rings out, echoing in the hills surrounding us. It's a normal sound with my dad letting bullets fly when he sees a stray cat on the property, or he goes hunting for turkeys with his brothers. The noise didn't come from the hills though; no, it came from down the road.

The roaring engine from the Chevy quiets to a rumble, idling as it comes to a stop. My gaze flies back to the porch where Percy stands, still pointing his shotgun toward the oversized blue truck and my breath catches.

There's blood splattered all over the back window, and I know deep down inside what's happened. You see, over the years there's been many threats from both sides, promising to shoot the other if the property lines were ever breached again. It never happened though; the threats were empty. At least I always thought they were.

The man glances to me next, his gun pointing to the ground. He sends me an irritated glare and stomps across his porch, slamming his front door as he passes through it and goes safely back inside.

He expects me to come get the truck from his front yard. The problem with that is I know my father's dead inside. He'd be yelling at the neighbor, shouting words full of revenge if he were still here with us.

I hate him, but he's all I've got. He's all I've had since I was six years old. Nine years of living this life—adapting and surviving—rolling with the punches dealt my way.

The rest of my father's family has been no help to me—ever. They're just like my father only a bunch of drunken cowards, worrying only about themselves. My dad's always been a survivor like me, until now.

The crushing feeling in my chest grows heavier. It begins spreading throughout and weighing down my body as I realize I have no one or nothing anymore. All because of this neighbor and his almighty shotgun. They've claimed their vengeance. Only now, I'm the one who's paying.

My eyes linger a moment too long on the scuffed lighter resting on my dad's pack of Marlboro Reds. He teased me so many times for coughing whenever I'd try to show off to him and smoke. The bright red gas can topped full with fuel sits at my feet. The italicized lettering spelling *flammable* cultivates an entirely new idea. It's one full of clarity; I know what I need to do to right this wrong.

On autopilot, my fingers pick up the faded zippo, palming it in my left hand and then lifting the gas can with my right. My frame moves on its own accord, practically possessed as it carries me toward the neighbor's house. It should take me longer to get there, but my quick strides carry me at a swift, determined pace. In no time at all, I'm at the run-down wooden structure, known as Percy Dickson's home.

I wonder if he was man enough to build it with his own two hands as well.

My feet continue to lead me over the trail circling around the residence. The fuel spills from the open gas can as I go, eventually stopping at the front door. I remain stoic, staring at the piece of oak that will lead me to my father's killer—to my retribution.

Flipping open the top of the lighter, my thumb switches over the metal, igniting a flame full of revenge. Percy may have kept his promise, but I'll be damned if he gets away unscathed.

My grip releases, dropping the cool metal to the ground beside me. Flickers of fiery yellows and blues dance next to my feet once the flame makes contact with the igniter. The fire spreads on its own mission, following the path of gas I left surrounding the entire residence.

Minutes pass with me standing and staring—entranced at the door—and waiting. My legs and face grow warm as smoke envelops the air around me, the house catching the brunt of the flame as it climbs toward the source that can feed its scorching desire to burn. As it all burns away, piece by piece, it sets me free.

Loud thumps grow near as Percy stumbles in his heavy construction boots, coughing behind the very door, I'm standing in front of. Like a moth seeking the brightest light, the doors handle jiggles, and then it stops. After a beat, with a loud cry from the man trapped, the metal begins to turn. He's seeking his freedom, but I'm not granting it; not today, not ever.

I blink, coming out of my daze and grab the handle, holding it in place. The metal scalds my palm, but I won't release it no matter how bad it burns. The man pounds on the other side of the door, screaming for help as I stand still, the fire flickering full of life beside me. Everything smolders around me, but for some reason, the heat doesn't harm me. It melts the skin on my palm—a reminder, no doubt—but I embrace it.

The old man struggles to breathe with the smoke and begins to burn alive. For the first time in a long time, I smile. The harsh stench of burning flesh brings me peace.

Once he's dead, I dump the remaining gasoline over the blue memory holding my father and light it up next. Everything burns away, and, in that moment, I vow to never look back. It's nothing but a fucking *nightmare*, after all.

CHAPTER 1

**You had me at a point where I
would've left the entire world behind
for you.**

- iglovequotes.net

BETHANY

I can't go home alone again; I need someone to numb the empty feeling of loneliness I get night after night. I hate letting myself get down like this as if I don't have anyone and it's the end of the world.

My mind slips back to the one-night stand I had three years ago, nearly to the day. It is the reason I'm feeling this way after all...

23

Nightmare.

He called me his daydream, whatever the hell that meant. It was probably the sweetest compliment I'd ever gotten from a man. It was a compliment, right?

It had to be.

God, he'd freaking worshiped my body that night too. He didn't care that I was high on percs. He'd growled and then laughed, and it was like seeing light for the first time in my life. That man made me feel, and for once, I wasn't trying to block out the pain. I wanted to see him, to remember him.

That story didn't have a happy ending for me like I'd foolishly let myself believe it would. I guess in a sense, it did, though; it brought me Maverick. However, it didn't turn out like I would've thought when I'd first laid eyes on Nightmare.

He was everything I wanted—the forbidden fruit—or so I thought. Boy, was I wrong, and I took one hell of a big bite.

The first thing I noticed about Nightmare that day we pulled into the shitty beatdown hotel parking lot wasn't the long, dark, wavy hair shadowing part of his face. Not even the black tattoos painting his skin or the thick, corded muscles overtaking his massive body.

It was the jagged silver strip running through one of the deep brown depths of his eyes. It started at the far corner of his eyebrow and sliced straight over his eyelid, nearly touching his nose. It was tiny but must've been a significant enough wound to change the color of one of his irises.

It was creepy and enthralling how he could stare me down like he could see completely through me. He wasn't fooled one bit by my loud mouth or the too-bright-too-fake smile that I always wore. He saw me for me; the plain-Jane, broken Bethany.

My life wasn't butterflies and rainbows. It was rough, and my mask was the only thing I owned that I could hide behind. Well, besides my best friend Princess. I hid behind her beauty a lot. She's not like me. She's strong and never lets anyone push her around, and it made me gravitate toward her like a dog to a bone.

My phone goes off, the ringtone blaring Avenged Sevenfold loudly. Grabbing it quickly, I take off into the bathroom, so it doesn't wake up Maverick. He fell asleep in the car after I'd picked him up on my way home from the restaurant. As much as I want him to be up and alert so I can spend some time with him, you don't wake a toddler at bedtime; you just don't do it.

"Hello?" It's whispered in a rush as I close the thin bathroom door and swipe across the screen to answer.

"Hey! Are you having sex? Oh, my God, why in the hell did you answer the phone?"

Her excited rush has me breathing out a giggle. "No. dumbass, Mav is sleeping, I was running."

"Why were you running if he's asleep?"

"Because my ringtone would've woken him up." With my little boy being around me every moment that I'm not working, I've forgotten what it's like to live without having a kid. Princess has her man and his little brother, who's not so little. More like a six-foot-three, eighteen-year-old that eats her out of the house practically.

"Oh, well, I feel like an ass."

"Don't, you'll figure it out someday."

She huffs, and in my mind, I can picture her rolling her eyes. "Viking still says he needs more time with me, to himself."

"Trust me, don't rush it. Enjoy each other while it's you guys. Maverick is the best thing that's ever happened to me, but it's not easy, Prissy."

"I must sound so ungrateful to you, and you're the one always over-working yourself."

"I don't mind; he's worth it. Plus, I don't like you sending me money. It makes me feel guilty, and I don't like that hanging over our friendship."

"I've known you my whole life, and that kid is my family too. It's nothing. Besides, what would I do with it anyhow?"

"I don't know, go grocery shopping maybe?"

She laughs, and it brings a smile to my face. I miss her so much. I miss the many nights we were off screwing around, just having fun together.

"You're still coming, right? No excuses?"

"It's your wedding, I wouldn't miss it."

"You promise?"

"For the millionth time; yes. I promise I'll be there, with bells on and Maverick at my side."

"Okay...it's just...well, I told you that it's going to be at the compound."

"We'll be fine. No one will remember me and nobody knows anything about Mav. He's the only concern I have."

"Night and Vike have grown close since Nightmare gave up his Nomad patch." She admits softly.

"He's not a Nomad anymore?" I trail off, not being able to hold back from asking about him. His name has my mind racing with the few memories I have of him.

"No, he's not; I thought I told you?"

"You, ah, haven't mentioned anything." I would remember if she had; I remember everything she says about him, and it's been kept to a minimal, even over a three-year period.

"Right, sorry. I don't want to bring him up. I just don't want you to be blindsided either. You're finally coming home after three years, and I don't want anything at all to go wrong. I need you here, standing beside me when I tie the knot."

"I still can't believe he asked you to marry him."

"Me either. From Viking, it was the last thing I ever expected, but he's calmed down a bit, you'll see."

"Doubt it," I reply immediately, and she laughs again.

"Okay, you're right. He's still a dick, but he's mine."

"He is. I'm so happy for you."

"And I'm so happy I'll see you guys. It's been six months since my last visit, and that's way too long."

"I know it is; I miss you." Tears crest and my throat begins to feel thick with emotion. I won't let her hear it though; I never do. "I have to work early, so I've got to get some sleep, but the promise is still good. In three days, I'll be heading your way."

"I love you."

"Love you, too."

"See you *soooon!*" she sings out happily, and I end the call with a smile.

I'm a bit leery because, in three days, I'll see the man who ruined me for anyone else. He's the man who broke my heart and also knows absolutely nothing about his three-year-old son. If he figures it out, he may also be the man who ends up killing me.

I switch my phone to silent and search out the box of cheap wine in my refrigerator. If I drink enough of it, it'll make me fall asleep without any dreams taking over my rest. The bad dreams are the worst. During the day, I can block everything out if I stay busy; but there's free reign on my mind when I'm sleeping.

That's one thing Maverick will never know—abuse as a child. I'll spend my last dying breath protecting him if I have to. I never cared about much before him; I would wash any memories I had away with alcohol and sex. If I was giving it up freely, then it could never be taken from me again.

28

Daydream

Now, I have this little man depending on me, so I have to be extra careful. That includes not leaving at night unless it's an emergency or for work. Like tonight, for example, I got off late, but I had to. I make so much more money when I work the night shift, and I need it if I'm taking time away to visit Princess.

I hate not being home to put Maverick to bed, too. That's usually our special time together, and I want him to have some sense of normal. Not just thinking that his mom is gone all the time working.

It's an unfair balance you have to find it seems. If you work too much, you're a bad parent for never being home with your kid. If you work too little and don't make enough money, your kid suffers by not having what they need. How on earth is that fucking fair? It's bullshit.

I down another glass of the cheap wine and the alcohol's trance kicks in, making me drowsier from my busy day. It's enough that if I go to sleep now, I don't think the dreams of my father will come to haunt me. I can never be sure though.

Peeling off my work uniform, I climb into bed in my bra and panties. I can shower in the morning; right now my body needs rest. Nightmare's silver and bronze gaze is the last thing I think of as I fall into a blissfully drunken sleep.

I miss him.

Sapphire Knight

CHAPTER 2

I broke my own heart loving you.

- Unknown

"Thanks, Barb."

She casts a friendly smile at me as she stands in the doorway and holds Maverick's hand in my direction. I reach my palm out to him, and he eagerly grabs it, a happy grin taking over his face, excited to be home. "You're welcome; you two have a safe trip and try to have some fun."

"We will. Enjoy your free time, too."

"Oh, I don't mind having Maverick around; he makes me feel young again." The older woman chuckles, waves, and heads toward her car.

Usually, I pick Mav up on my way home, but Barbara was out running errands and saved me the trip. It worked out perfectly, too; it gave me enough time to get my car loaded up with everything for our trip. My nerves were kind enough to show up as well. I was hoping to leave them behind, but, apparently, they didn't feel the same way. Hopefully, the drive will chill me out some.

It looks like we're going across the country or something when it's only four hours away. Anyone with kids knows that you have to pack everything but the kitchen sink practically, to keep almost-three-year-olds busy, especially at a wedding. Bikers or not, I don't want to bring too much attention to us, or any attention at all.

"Hey, buddy." Pulling him in for a snuggle, I wrap my arms around. "I missed you today. Are you ready for our trip to see Aunt Prissy?"

"Yes! She has gummies?"

Six months since her trip here and he still talks about her spoiling him with gummy bears. He was in such a sugar rush during her visit; I thought I was going to strangle her. He doesn't need a grandma to feed him sugar on visits when he has Princess.

"Knowing her, probably. The car's all ready. Is there anything I'm forgetting?" I made him pick out some toys to fit in one backpack, no more. He tried to tell me we needed to bring his toy box, but it wasn't happening.

He taps his chin, looking around the living room.

He's so freaking adorable with his black locks he gets from both Nightmare and me, along with big brown eyes from his father that haunt my memories. Hopefully, no one looks close enough, or they'll be able to figure out whose blood runs through his body pretty easily.

"Ummm...snacks?" Surprise, surprise; snacks was one of the kid's first words.

"Got 'em."

"Ummm...Mr. Bwair?"

"Got Mr. Bear, too."

"Ummm..." He looks at me, his eyebrow raising and shrugs.

"That's what I was thinking. First trip this far away, I'm sure we'll figure it out soon enough."

Yeah, so I ended up forgetting my cash, and two hours down the road had to turn around when I stopped to get gas and only found a twenty in my purse. A four-hour road trip turned into eight hours, and let's just say, Maverick was not amused in the slightest, at my mishap.

"I thought you'd never get here!" Princess squeezes me tightly, again. She's done it three times since she opened her front door.

"God, me too. Just be glad the kid passed out, or you'd be ready for us to leave already."

"No way, I love the little guy. I was hoping he'd be awake. I'm thinking once Viking gets around Maverick, he'll want to have some kids of our own."

"Trust me, he was super grouchy the hour before he finally gave in. His favorite word was 'NO.' I'm pretty sure he said it fifty times and threw so many damn action figures, they'll forever be lost in my car."

She laughs, finding enjoyment in my mini ride of torture. Payback—one day she'll be calling me, flipping out because her kids being a brat and then I'll laugh. It's what best friends do.

"Well, hopefully after some rest, he'll be in a better mood tomorrow. He can run after Odin and get some exercise too."

"That sounds good to me. Now, please tell me you have some wine?"

"I have vodka and OJ; will that do the trick?"

"Definitely, hook it up." I follow her into the kitchen and take a seat at the table. "Thank you for letting us stay with you, I hope we don't bother you though. Mav still gets up really early."

"Of course, I wouldn't want you anywhere else. And besides, I've stayed with you, and he's a lot quieter than I'd expect."

"Yeah, cartoons and a bowl of cereal and he's pretty calm. He needs time to wake up and get going."

"Just like his mom." She winks, and I smile. I love being here, even after a long trip and an hour of kid yelling to make it here.

"So what's the plan for tomorrow exactly?"

I'm nervous, but at the same time, I'm excited to see the guys. I don't expect them to remember me, but I could never forget the rough group of bikers. They're Princess' family now, and I'm so happy she's found her tribe. I always knew she belonged in the MC world. Her parents and brother were deep into it; she just needed the right piece to make her fit as well. That turned out to be Viking, and he's the President of the entire club. Go figure.

She sets the glass in front of me, taking the seat to my left and sips her own drink. "Pretty much just hang out. We're having a barbecue at the club to welcome some visiting members, mostly the Nomads coming in for the wedding, but both clubs will be there."

"The hybrids and the Oath Keepers?"

"Yes, but don't call them hybrids; the Widow Makers were patched over to the Oath Keepers. Oath Keepers essentially took over the Widow Maker name. They let a small charter keep the patch in South Carolina, but Viking's club here is Oath Keepers. You already know that much though. He works with Ares a lot; they're practically BFFs now."

"That's crazy, considering they hated each other with a passion in the beginning."

"I know, but they both love my father, and, thankfully, were able to bond over him and work through their shit. It makes things so much easier."

"Okay, so the same guys that were with your dad and Ares are under Ares, and the others belong to Viking's charter?"

"Right, that's why we moved a little ways out of town. This way they can each have separate clubs."

"Jesus, y'all must run Texas by now."

"With the size of the clubs, we're definitely dominant in this state."

"Listen to you, no doubt a President's wife."

"Ol' lady." She winks. "And it has taken time to get there, believe me."

"You fit so well, though. Who'd have thought this is how your life would turn out?"

"I know, and the freaky part is, I've never been happier. I wish my mom was here to be a part of it all."

"She is, Princess. That woman wouldn't let you out of her sight when it comes to the club. I know she's looking down on you every day."

"I hope so." She wipes a stray tear away as the front door opens with Viking and Odin piling through.

"Well, there's trouble." Viking acknowledges me, walking to his woman and giving her a blistering kiss.

"Hey." I smile, and Odin bends over, giving me a half hug.

I've met him before; Viking makes him come with Princess on each visit. He says it's to keep Odin busy, but we all know it's to protect Princess if she ever needed it. He may only be eighteen, but he's a tank—a lethal one at that—and Princess is the closest thing he has in his life now to a mom, older sister, female friend, etc.

"'Sup Bethany, how was the drive?" Odin nods, heading to the fridge.

Daydream

"Long; glad to finally be here."

"Bet." He nods again, pulling out a pack of lunch meat and some mayo, heading to the counter to make a sandwich.

Viking detaches from Princess after a moment, "Where's this mini version my ol' lady won't stop talking to me about?"

"He's asleep, but you'll meet him tomorrow." And Maverick will no doubt be curious with Viking. He already thinks Odin is the greatest thing since peanut butter and jelly because he spins him around a million times like he enjoys.

"Good. I'm hitting the shower," he grumbles, glancing at Princess. They have their own language it seems; they always have.

"Night, Viking." I smile politely, and he salutes me, heading toward their bedroom.

He's not a man of many words, but, from what I remember, none of the bikers talk much. Kind of weird for them to have a barbecue. Do they just stand around quiet, drinking beer? I will no doubt laugh if I see it happen tomorrow because it's so not what you'd expect to see with a bunch of bikers.

I'd met most of them a few times before I found out I was pregnant and moved away. They stuck together out in public, and when I was with Nightmare, no one bothered him. Some of Princess' dad's bikers had shown up the next morning, but they were all talking about a car when I made it out of the hotel room.

I wonder if Ruger will be there. He was friendly; I think he liked me, too. He went swimming with us once

37

and was pretty funny. He'd attempted to get fresh, too, but I shot him down right away. I'd only ever had eyes for one brother.

"I should get some sleep, too. Maverick will be up early, and I'll need energy to keep up with him tomorrow around everyone."

"He'll have a few other kids to play with, too. London and Cain's kids will be there, and their youngest daughter is the same age, I think."

"Oh, good. It'll be nice to have a beer and some adult conversation that I actually want to have. I get so tired of the assholes hitting on me at the restaurant."

"I can imagine, but don't be surprised if the guys hit on you tomorrow, too."

"But, I'll have my son with me."

She snorts, "*Pahleese,* a little boy won't scare any of them off. They'll take one look at those hips and won't care about anything else."

"That's what I'm afraid of," I mumble, and her grin falls.

"You'll have fun, I promise."

"I know, don't worry about me. I'm here for you, remember?"

"You don't know how much it means to me that you are."

"No worries, woman. Now go attend to your fiancé. I'm pretty sure he was sending you silent messages with the looks he gave you on the way to y'all's room."

"He's insatiable." She laughs, and Odin makes a gagging sound.

"Don't wanna hear that shit," he says around a mouthful of sandwich, and Princess picks up an ink pen that was on a notebook in the middle of the table. He looks at us, and she throws the pen at his forehead.

He ducks, cursing, and we both laugh. She knows how to keep him on his toes, I'm sure of it. If Prissy and Viking do ever have kids of their own, the kids are in for a ride no doubt.

"Goodnight, you guys, see you tomorrow." I climb to my feet, and Princess follows.

"Yep, I'll be the pretty one."

"Oh my God, he's made your head get bigger since I left," I retort.

"Shut up! Love you."

"Love you." I squeeze her one last time and close the door to the guest room they're letting us stay in. It's perfect for us, too; we have a small, private bathroom and a king-sized bed to share.

I take a quick, super-hot shower to scrub the road grime off and then hit the sack, grateful to be snuggled next to my son in my best friend's house. I missed being around her so much; it even feels good to be back to the place I grew up, even if my life wasn't the greatest.

Sapphire Knight

CHAPTER 3

**Yeah, I'm hurting but on goes the
mascara and lip gloss. That's right,
I'll be the prettiest fucking
wreck you've ever seen.**
- Unknown

"Hey, Bethany," Viking grumbles while sitting on the couch watching cartoons with my son. "Why's Maverick look so much like my homeboy?"

My chest tightens at his words.

He means Nightmare, his brother. I knew I never should've come here; at least, not with my son. Princess has kept my secret for which I'm beyond grateful. Honestly, I never expected her to be able to keep it from her ol' man and for this amount of time too.

Deep down I've been waiting for the angry pounding on my front door, but it hasn't come. My big secret could really stir some shit up between them if Viking were to find out who Maverick belongs to. With their wedding in the works, that's the last thing I want to do. I would never want to hurt or cause trouble between them.

The thing is, Princess doesn't know just how much has been kept in the dark. I've misled my best friend, and I hate myself for it. At the time, it was all I had. I was hurt by Nightmare's words, and I didn't want anything to do with him after.

That's a lie. I've thought of him countless times over the years. I have wanted him, every fucking piece of him, but he wouldn't want my son—our son.

I still remember his words like they were said yesterday.

"I'm sterile and clean," he rasps against my neck. "I told you this already, the other night when we fucked."

I've been sick each morning since that first night, too. I can't get ahold of Princess because Viking has her trapped in his room, and her mom never answered her door when I went over. I have no one to talk to about this.

My own mother would just tell me that I'm a whore and kick me out. She doesn't have time for me; she only cares about her husband. She's made it abundantly clear many times.

Naturally, I ran back to Nightmare. I'm scared. The doctor says I could be pregnant, but how do I say the words out loud to an outlaw? He's a Nomad for Christ's sake. I seriously doubt he's the type to win a father of the year award; even I know that much.

"You're sure?" I mutter, my breath catching, waiting for his deep voice to offer some kind of reassurance. But he doesn't. He breaks my heart instead because I know the truth, I just have to hear him say it.

He plunges inside me deeply from behind as he grumbles, "Of course. The fuck I'm gonna do with a kid? I'm not father material, none of us are. I wouldn't be fuckin' you bareback like this if I was gonna knock you up. Clearly, I like my freedom."

My eyes crest with tears because, just like I knew his words were going to sting, I also know inside that the doctor is right. I have a little life growing inside me. It was created by this man—the one taking my body right now—and he wants nothing to do with any of it.

He wants to take his pleasure and leave me with the consequences.

"Right, I'm just being paranoid or something." I swallow as he pumps into me again. No matter how good he feels filling me, I won't get off. He basically told me that if I were pregnant, he wouldn't want the baby. He wouldn't want a piece of me.

No one does. My father abused me in ways I would never wish for anyone to experience. My mother hates me; I'm a burden that she's counting the days to be rid of. And now the father of my own child doesn't want the one thing I'm able to offer him- life.

"Or sumthin'," he agrees, continuing with his pursuit of pleasure.

Silent tears trail over my heated cheeks, but I don't utter a word. He won't know my pain, no one will. I'll be the very thing I've needed my entire life. I'll be strong.

Princess thinks I told Nightmare that I was pregnant, and he pushed me away. It's why she hates him. She's never said it out loud; she won't since it's Viking's brother and club business. It's not her place to tear him down for his choices, even if I am her best friend. She respects her ol' man, and I respect her for it. Not only that, but it's a lie. She came to that conclusion on her own, and I let her run with it.

Nightmare doesn't have any idea that he has a kid out there. At least not with me, anyhow. Who knows if there are others out in the world. I was so damn naïve to believe him the first time we were together, and he told me he couldn't have kids. More like he was in denial and I proved him wrong.

They can all hate me for my decisions, and that's fine. I've made my choices, and I've lived with them every damn day of Maverick's life. Would I go back and do it differently if I could?

Maybe, but I doubt it.

I had my reasons for keeping him a secret, and, at the time, I felt like I was doing what I had to. Time only built my confidence stronger in my decision. Nightmare never looked for me. For all I know, he never even asked about me. I was nothing, probably not even a memory.

I don't want that in my kid's life, someone who won't remember him. Maverick is everything. He won't have a life like I had. He'll be surrounded by people who love him, and will protect him.

I'm surprised to hear Night isn't a Nomad any longer considering his freedom was so important to him after all. Things change, I suppose. I'm guessing that having Viking as the President of his own Charter most likely has a lot to do with it.

I hate lying to Viking. He's never done anything to me personally, and he takes care of my best friend. However, the safety of my child is everything, and if Nightmare wanted me dead for keeping this from him, the club wouldn't even bat an eyelash, and Mav would be left without a mother.

I shrug, glancing to the side, and deflect, "I think he looks like his mom. Lucky kid, since I'm hot."

Vike snorts, turning back to the show.

My reply worked...for now. But if Viking can pick him out first thing in the morning, then I may have a harder time when Mav is around people that see his father every day and have a chance to really get a good look at him.

If Princess wasn't so damn important to me, I never would've come here. There's no reason to after all. My mother doesn't know about Maverick; she wouldn't care, and that's fine with me. She's not a good person and doesn't deserve to know my son. And wherever my father ended up, I hope it's six feet under, and he suffered.

The only one I would've gone out of my way to have in his life would've been Mona—Princess' mom. I loved her so much; she was a great mom. She died of cancer a few years ago, so having her in Mav's life isn't an option.

I was too broke and struggling to make ends meet with Maverick; I wasn't able to attend her funeral. I hated it, but I know she would've understood. She was just like that—always caring for and worrying about others.

She'd have been pissed at me if I'd tried to travel and then something had happened to me or the baby on the road. I said my piece to her at the time, and I still talk to her randomly. She may not really be there, but I talk to her like I believe she is.

"You're wearing that?" My mouth falls open as Princess comes out of her room.

"Yeah, it's hot."

"Exactly, you'll bake in black leather."

"They're shorts, I'll be fine. Besides, the halter top doesn't have a back to it." She spins around, and my mouth drops open again. She's straight up doin' the hootchie momma thing.

"Viking!" I mutter and tilt my head toward my friend. He'll let her out the door like this?

He glances at her, a pleased smirk taking over his lips. He's as bad as she is.

"How do you go anywhere? Won't he chop off guys' heads?" Her ol' man is nutso when it comes to jealousy, and that's the last thing I want myself or my kid to see at a barbecue.

"They know better," he declares, his voice confident and stern. I wouldn't fuck with him.

She shrugs, waving it off. "They either stare at my face or look at the ground. I could be naked, and no one would comment."

I hear a growl come from Viking's direction.

"Jesus." I shake my head. It's a wonder he has any club brothers left at this rate.

"Is that what you're wearing?" She points toward my boobs, flicking her gaze over my dress a few times and basically cringes.

"Yes."

"Since when do you wear maxi dresses?"

"It's one of the halfway decent things I can get away with. Regular dresses? Maverick thinks it's hilarious to grab the skirt part and take off running. This is long enough and stretchy."

"You look like a hobo. It's definitely the wrong size for you."

"Gee, thank you, assface."

She giggles. "Come on, I have something you can borrow."

"Uh no. I have hips, remember? Having a baby changed some things."

She rolls her eyes and grabs my hand to drag me to her room. "In your case, it finally gave you an ass."

I end up coming out in a different dress, surprise, surprise. This one's a sun dress though with stretchy material. Fingers crossed my kid doesn't flash my new ass to anyone today. I expect to see someone's boobs at some point, it being a biker compound, but none of those body parts need to belong to myself.

After letting her screw with my hair and makeup which I bitch about the entire time, but secretly love, we're finally ready. It helps having other people around to distract Maverick. I don't usually have time to do anything special to my hair before work besides a quick ponytail. Mom duties overshadow hairstyles when it's just the two of us.

I smear a healthy coat of sunscreen all over my son and grab his backpack full of Matchbox trucks and action figures. All he needs is some snacks and a little dirt to play in, and he'll be one happy little boy.

"Ready?" Smiling, I fix his black tank top I have paired with army green camo shorts and chucks. He looks freaking adorable as usual. It pays to have a cool mom on your side.

"Ummm...yep."

The 'ummm' thing drove me a little nuts at first, but the pediatrician said it's normal for kids to pick a favorite word. Right now, Maverick's favorite happens to be 'Um.' Guess it's better than 'mine.'

"He'll fit in just fine with the other biker kids." Princess shoots me a look. She knows I'm tripping out inside over seeing Nightmare after so long. Even being separated for a while, she can still read me like an open book.

I nod, we're good. At least that's what I keep telling myself. Fake it til you make it has been my life motto thus far. Why stop now?

"Follow behind Odin, and Viking will let the brother at the gate know you're with us, okay?"

"All right. Just give me a sec to strap him in his seat, and we'll be right behind you." I look to Odin, and he gives me thumbs-up. For being raised by a badass, he doesn't usually reflect it.

"Later kid." He holds his fist out, and Maverick fist bumps him.

Only one morning being here and Odin's already teaching my son to fist bump. Viking does the same, letting Mav fist bump him, too, before heading out the door, and then we're off.

I've never been to Viking's compound before. It was built after I left, and, well, I'm amazed. I was expecting it to be a crappy little building in the middle of nowhere to hold a bunch of rowdy bikers, but it's not. Not even a little bit.

Princess' house is on the back side of the property, so it's really close to the actual building, but you have to drive in a sort of circle around a bunch of trees to get there. Viking did it on purpose. He wanted her close to him, but not too close, so if any shit ever went down, she wouldn't be harmed. He can cut through the trees on foot to get to her, but vehicles and motorcycles have to drive around. It's perfect actually.

They stop for a second to talk to the member standing at the gate, and then we all roll through, the biker nodding to each of us as we pass. He's young, probably closer to Odin's age. I've never seen him before. As we pass by slowly, I catch his name patch, *Bronx*. Definitely never met him; I'd remember the name.

I watch Maverick in my rearview mirror waving at the guy. Instead of acting cool and ignoring him, Bronx breaks out in a grin and waves back. I won't lie; it brings a cheesy smile to my face. Maybe today won't be so bad after all. Lord knows we're about to find out.

CHAPTER 4

**Until you cross the bridge of your
insecurities, you can't begin to
explore your possibilities.**

- Tim Fargo

"I haven't seen him yet." I glance around again making sure Nightmare hasn't suddenly appeared. The place is littered with men in leather cuts visiting with each other, but none resemble the man I remember.

"He was on a run this week; he'll be rolling in soon with Chaos."

"Who's Chaos?"

"Another member." Princess winks, being a smartass.

She failed to mention yesterday that he wasn't even in town; it would've saved me a lot of immediate worrying. What if I'm spazzing out for nothing? He could show up and completely ignore me. It never crossed my mind before, but what if he shows up with another woman?

Holy shit, how could I not think of that? I'm not with anyone, so I automatically picture him with no one as well. I'm a freaking idiot. It's been years; he could have his own wife!

No. He likes his freedom; he flat out told me that. He won't be married—he *can't* be.

Fuck.

"It's not what you're thinking, it was a gig."

She knows what I'm thinking? I hope she can't tell. "A what?"

"You know, a job. He still plays. One thing he didn't give up over the time you've been away is his sticks."

What the hell is she talking about? Sticks?

"What's he play, exactly?"

"Wait, you don't know?" Her eyebrows raise, and I shake my head. "He's a drummer. All this time, I thought you knew that about him."

"Nope, I had no clue. We don't exactly talk about him, you know."

"I'm sorry; I try not to bring him up to you. I don't want to hurt you after the way he treated you and all."

I nod. Not sure what else to say right now. I thought he was just a biker, but now that I'm here, I find out he's not even a Nomad anymore. He's a drummer, and I had no idea. I feel like I don't know him at all. We fucked, and I fell. I didn't need to know anything to want him and then let my heart get broken in the same breath.

"Are you okay?" My friend's worried gaze meets mine.

"Yeah, I'm fine." Lies.

Brush it off, B.

"Maybe you should have a beer. I'm here. I'll help keep an eye on Maverick; besides, he's completely fine with London's daughter. She won't let anything happen to either one of them."

"It's kind of early; I was going to wait until later when we eat. I only have one beer if I have to drive somewhere."

"Listen to you, all responsible. I'm so fucking proud of you, Bethany."

"I have to be and thank you."

"Well, if you want to drink, go ahead. We can always walk home if we need to or one of the Prospects can drive us. You're safe here, try to relax and let yourself have a little bit of fun."

"You're sure?"

"Yes. I know you can't be the crazy girl you used to be, which is completely fine- I understand and admire you. But you can cut loose here; you know I'll never let anything happen to you or Maverick."

"Thank you." I let a pent-up breath free.

I can have a beer now and then another later when we eat. I'll be able to be momma and still function, but the alcohol will help calm my nerves a bit. No hard stuff, it's been forever since I drank tequila and the last thing I want to do is pray to the porcelain god in the morning. That would be a train wreck, no doubt.

The sound of motorcycles arriving catches my attention as multiple loud exhausts rumble into the parking lot. Three bikes come to a stop, and I know who it is before he has a chance to climb off.

Exterminator swings his leg over, his back patch still reading Nomad. At least there's one thing that hasn't changed. Another man, a bit older comes to stand beside him, and I'm guessing that must be Chaos. He's gorgeous, distinguished, I'd say mid-fifties and fit. Built like a football player with a look of pure trouble.

Then comes my demise; I can feel him, and he's nowhere near me. My gaze finds powerful thighs, still the size of small tree trunks like I remember. Surprising, too, after the attack Princess had told me about. I figured they'd be skinny from the damage, hidden away by jeans, but that's clearly not the case.

He turns around to grab something off his bike and the deep brown, shoulder length waves I loved running my fingers through are gone. In their place are long dreads, unruly but neat in a sense. And sure enough, a pair of drummer sticks stuck in one of his back pockets. How did I never notice them before?

His shirt sleeves are cut. Big gaping holes show off his arms that've only gotten larger with time. He's a beast, and I missed that body something fierce. The only man I didn't faze out when he took my body. I was present with him, I felt everything, I wanted everything.

"Shit," Princess whispers beside me. "I wasn't expecting them until a little later."

I blow out another breath. "How about that beer now?" I ask, watching Night light up a cigarette. That hasn't changed either. I can still smell him—leather, smoke, and spice with a touch of exhaust and wind mixed in. The guys chuckle beside him and his lips tip at the corners, always a broody bastard. Being that hot shouldn't be allowed on an asshole.

"Good idea."

One thing that didn't escape my perusal is that he was alone on his bike. Just as I was hoping, too, whether I want to admit it or not.

"Come on." She takes off toward a few large tubs filled with ice and various beverages. "We have some really good moonshine that we get from Alabama, wanna do a shot?"

"No, it'll put me on my ass. Maybe later after I've eaten and absolutely no tequila." She laughs, knowing tequila turns me into a hellion.

I check on Maverick as we walk, but he's content surrounded by toys, a juice box, and a couple small kids. I'm glad he's busy; it'll wear him out for a nap later. At this rate, I'll most likely need one, too; my nerves are fried already.

She cracks open a Smirnoff for herself and hands me a Bud Light. It's cold and refreshing. I don't miss drinking itself, just hanging out with friends and not caring about anything.

"We can set up the food. I'm sure everyone's getting hungry by now."

"Is this what you always do?"

"What? Set up the tables?"

"Yeah, just take care of everyone and help take care of the club?"

"Yeah, this is what an ol' lady does, especially since Vike is the President. It puts more on me."

"You like it?"

"I love it. I understand now why my mom was so lost when my dad started keeping her away from the club. They become your family, and this," she waves around her, "becomes your whole life."

"I know you're involved with stuff, from the calls and your visits, but I didn't know it was like this. It reminds me more of a reunion than a rowdy barbecue."

"They have their moments, trust me. Today is a family event. They know it's to celebrate me and Viking, so they'll tone it down for me and the families visiting."

I catch her wrist, so she pauses and meets my gaze. "I want you to know, I truly am happy for you. I always wanted you to find your place and be happy."

Her grin's a little shaky as she pulls me in for a hug, "Thanks, B. Hopefully, someday you have it too."

"I hope so." It leaves me on a whisper, but it's true. It never hit me so hard as it has in this moment.

I want this.

Maybe not being a Prez's ol' lady, but the sense of family, of belonging, of purpose. I love being a mom, but I want Maverick to grow up surrounded by people who love him, not just a few, but many. I want him to have a family, people who love him that I never had.

A few bikers stand around in the kitchen, no doubt quietly speaking about business of some sort. They glance at us briefly as we unintentionally interrupt them.

"Hey, Torch, will you carry that potato salad for me?" Princess requests as she opens the fridge door and gestures to the top shelf.

"You got it, boss." He grabs the massive plastic bowl that most likely weighs fifty pounds knowing Princess.

He's new to me. She's told me about the guys, but I haven't seen a lot of them before. Her description of him was right. He reminds me of the Terminator—menacing, but hot. Torch is supposed to be one of Viking's oldest friends, and a biker around here called Blaze is supposed to be his cousin. I haven't seen him yet, though.

"Thanks. Bethany, will you get the paper plates and forks?"

"Yes, ma'am." I grin, and she rolls her eyes.

They head out of the room, while I load up a plastic bag with a bunch of plates and utensils. She said forks, but may as well get everything; I know she'll ask for it next. The other bikers in here ignore me, going back to their chat and I do my best to not overhear anything. The last thing I want is to be putting my nose in other people's business.

Once the bag's full, I make my way to the hall that leads out the club's back door. I hate not having Maverick in my sight, but Princess says I can trust

London. She'd never let either of us get hurt, so I believe her.

My heads in la-la land as I walk the long hall, not paying attention to the shadow in a passing doorway. The shadow sees me, however.

My wrist is snatched in a tight grip, my gaze flying to the source of strength.

"Bethany?" he utters deeply, and the air catches in my lungs. How could I not know he was standing there? *Fuck.* My pussy clenches from his voice alone.

He gazes at me, confused and a little surprised to see me. I'm guessing that I'm the last person he was expecting to be walking around their clubhouse.

"Ummm." I begin to stutter, the word instantly making me think of Maverick. I know where he gets it from now. Shit.

"You're here?" His voice swallows me whole, coating my body in tingles as his other hand finds my cheek. His palm's rough and big, easily covering part of my face and jaw with warmth.

How does he expect me to speak when he's touching me like this? I could barely say anything before when I didn't hate him. And lack of words has never been an issue for me; if anything, it was always the opposite.

His touch is everything—caring and controlling—just the way I liked it before. The heat from his palm ignites my body in sensory overload. I want him to feel me everywhere, rub me all over.

"Yes?" I nod, a little unsure of what he even said. I know he spoke and I need to give him a response; to what, who knows? I can't think, I only feel him and take in his features.

He's aged a touch, but nothing too noticeable. The few lines from his ever-present glare and his time out on the road have gotten slightly more pronounced, but that's about all. His hair's throwing me a bit. It's so much longer, and I've never cared for dreads, but I like them on him. He wears the look well, reminding me of one of the guys you see in a heavy metal video— forbidden and wild.

"Where have you been?" He's angry; I can hear it in his voice. He's pissed over something. Over me leaving? No way; he has no reason to be. I was the one who left hurt and upset, not the other way around.

"B?" Princess comes into the hall, a concerned gaze at Nightmare's hand on me. Her wake never falters, coming to me immediately and grabbing onto my free hand, holding the plastic bag in a death grip. "Come on Bethany, I need you to help me." Her eyes snap to Nightmare's, full of her own warning. She can't say anything to him; it's not her place in the club, but she can tell her ol' man if something bothers her.

He drops his hands from me, releasing my cheek and wrist. Taking a step back, his gaze shutters, and without another word, he watches my best friend cart me toward the door. He never says anything, and part of me wishes he would stop us, while the other can't stop thinking of how it felt when he touched me.

How did I ever think I could come back here and he wouldn't affect me? I've never been that strong. I am for Maverick, but never for myself and never when it comes to Nightmare.

Maverick.

59

"Mav—" I begin, and Princess cuts me off.

"Is fine. I checked on him. I don't think Night has seen him yet."

"Thank you."

"Of course; I have your back."

"We should go."

"Already? Please stay. What if you go back to my house and take a breather?"

"Okay, I can do that. Maverick will probably be ready for a nap soon anyhow. I just need some space from him." I nod at the back door.

"I've been with Viking for a while now; I get it. They have a way of overtaking everything, nearly smothering you at times."

"Exactly." I set the bag down and toss the half-full beer in the metal trash bin. Smother is a good word to use whenever I'm near him; consumed would work as well.

Collecting my kid and his stuff, we get out of there as quickly and quietly as possible, not wanting to draw any attention.

It doesn't take long before Maverick's down for a nap, and I'm lying beside him, tears flooding my face. I was a fool to think I wouldn't be that messed up at seeing Night. It's been years—actual years since I saw his face and heard his voice—yet he has this control over me within minutes. Not only did he suck me right back in, but he twisted my heart all over again knowing that the innocent little boy playing right outside is unwanted by his own father.

Fuck you, Nightmare!

Daydream

My own tiredness sets in, and I succumb to sleep. Unfortunately, there's not enough alcohol in my system to drown out memories that like to torment me in my dreams—my nightmares.

Sapphire Knight

CHAPTER 5

**And the stars blinked as they
watched her carefully, jealous
of the way she shone.**

- Atticus

NIGHTMARE

My leg aches as I stand on that side for too long causing me to shift and relieve some pressure.

Fuckin' Lion.

Of course, I'd be the motherfucker who was attacked out of the brothers. That's neither here nor there; it's been forever since that fucked-up day. I need to let that shit go already. I've gotten a lot of my strength and movement back with a shit ton of work, but my leg will never be the same as it used to be. Guess that's what happens when a Lion decides to use you as an appetizer. I damn sure can't run for shit; guess if I'm being chased I'll have to shoot instead of run.

Stupid fuckin' cartel. Those bastards always fuck shit up. I still think we should find every one of those sneaky bastards and light them up. It'd solve a lot of problems, but the brothers think I'm crazy.

'I'm angry, and they get it.' They don't get shit. They weren't attacked, their lives weren't completely changed. Thank fuck it didn't mess with me playing too. It screwed me out of riding for about a year. Hell, the doc said not to ever ride again. Fuckin' idiot, like I wasn't gonna ride again. I told him to get the fuck outta here with that shit. I'm not a pussy; I'm not giving up my bike.

I lean against the wall a bit more, my sticks digging into my ass, reminding me that they're there. I usually stick them back there if I have a gig and then forget about them. I played last night with a local band. Chaos and Ex came out to show some support, then we got pretty fucked up on whiskey afterward. Damn sure beat this barbecue going on right now.

Don't get me wrong, Viking's my brother, and I have his back one hundred and fifty percent. I even think Princess is good for him. It's not them; it's Bethany. She was the last person I was expecting to see.

When Vike first announced he was getting hitched, of course, I instantly thought of B stopping through. Princess hasn't said a word about her since she split. One minute she was here in my bed and the next she'd left town. The bitch doesn't even visit her best friend. I thought maybe they stopped talking or something.

Then to top it off, she only says two words to me. The last time I saw her, I thought for sure she was into me. She would stare at me like I was a goddamn puppy or some shit. She's a prime example of why I don't let women in too close. The club is my family; they're all I need.

There's just one little detail that's driving me crazy. So much so, that I find myself making my way to Viking's office. He's not supposed to be working this week since he's getting married, but I saw him sneak into his office. He's either in there for some quiet or because he's a damn control freak and can't stand letting other people handle shit for him.

Opening the door, I slide in quickly and shut it, so no one knows we're in here.

"Brother?" He glances at me, eyebrow raised.

"Saw Bethany."

He nods, taking his seat behind the desk. I do the same, sitting in one of the broken-in leather seats opposite him. We're not big talkers the two of us. We both think a lot before opening our mouths, so our conversations are usually short and straight to the point. This is one time I don't know how to bring something up, though.

Very few members know how I feel about Bethany. Vike found out by pure luck when he was on the hunt for Princess. I slipped up a few times and my brother caught on. The others are like a group of gossiping broads and too wrapped up in themselves to pay attention to my shit.

Viking, not so much. We're broody fuckers who often growl at people more than we speak, so he pretty much knew by the second look I gave the chick that I was planning on fucking her.

"She's here for the wedding." He takes a healthy gulp of beer.

"Figured."

After a few moments of silence, he speaks again. "That all brother?"

"No."

He nods again, staring me down, but I don't know how to sugarcoat shit, so I stay quiet for a few more minutes, making shit awkward. Eventually, he goes back to working on whatever he was doing when I interrupted him, and I blurt out the thoughts bothering me.

"She had a kid with her." So what if I followed her when Princess took her. I wasn't about to let her escape that easily. Then she grabbed up a little boy. That had my step faltering and letting her go without me interfering. Now I can't stop thinking about it.

"Yeah, I met him this morning."

"First time?"

"Yep."

"She married too?"

He barks out a laugh. "This is B we're talkin' about. She doesn't have a fucking husband."

I let loose a relieved breath, and he grows serious again, seeing how much the thought was eating me up. I was racking my brain trying to think if I'd seen a ring on her hand, but fuck, I was too distracted. One look in those eyes of hers, and I couldn't give a fuck about anything else in the moment. I wanted to rip her clothes off and sink balls deep into her tight pussy right there in the hallway. I wanted to demand that she tell me why she left and why she hasn't come back sooner. Maybe make it hurt a little and punish her ass for keeping me waiting so long.

"She bring an ol' man with her, too?" Not that it matters; if anything, he'd get his feelings hurt by the way she still looks at me.

"No. Just her and the kid. Maybe you should talk to my Cinderella; she'd know the shit you're asking." Her name's Princess, and he calls her Cinderella. Fucker has a shoe fetish now, too, from what I hear. Not my business, but kinda ironic.

"She won't tell me anything. Your ol' lady's harder than some of the bikers I've met in my life." It's the truth too; the bitch is cold as ice toward me.

He cracks a tiny grin. "Fuck, yeah, she is." He finishes off his bottle and tosses it in the small wastebasket beside the desk. "Not sure I can give you the answers you're wanting, brother."

"Those were the main ones I had. How long's she staying? I'm guessing she'll beat feet back outta here pretty quick?"

"You have a week."

Huffing, I drum my fingers along my thigh. "They've stayed friends this whole time, then?"

"Yeah, they have, man. Cinderella visits her and shit."

"That's where her and Odin go then." It's not a question. Details are just starting to click into place, and I want him to confirm I'm correct.

"That's right, brother."

"Appreciate it." Nodding my thanks, I leave him to his business.

He shakes my hand. "Good luck."

I have a feeling I need more than luck this time. One thing that running into Bethany has showed me, is that she wasn't happy to see me. She was surprised, but not pleased, and that's a problem.

I head back toward the other brothers, grabbing a beer on my way. Viking will give it to me straight if he thinks I'm stupid for asking about her. I can trust him. He didn't mention anything about me being a fool or that I should keep my space, so that's something.

Do I really want to get involved with her again, though, now that she has a kid? Baby daddy drama and all that shit in tow. I'd end up throwing the bastard in a dumpster and lighting it up if he gave her any kind of grief with me around. Not sure she wants that sorta shitshow in her life.

It could be my chance at having a brat, though, if it were to work out. One thing that's always ate away at me was not being able to have kids someday. I enjoy my freedom a lot; but hell, I want to have my own family eventually.

I usually fall back on it as a way to push people away. You're less likely to get hurt by anyone if they think you never want anything with them more than a quick fuck. I'll be real, for a while tapping pussy and riding was exactly what I wanted. I'm getting older now and am no longer a Nomad, and having a family isn't looking like a hindrance anymore. Quick fucks are great. I love that shit, but I want to have a son to carry on my name and my blood. I want to have the chance to be a good father, unlike my own old man.

Princess has everything set up all nice and organized so everyone can load up their plates. She stands on the opposite side, helping the younger kids pick out what they want to eat. She's always around the club, helping out and making sure everyone has what they need. Except for me, she usually pretty well ignores me. I don't know why. I've never wronged her in any way, and I'd like to think of myself as being close with her ol' man.

Grabbing a plate, I fall into line behind the kids. Sure, I could grab what I want and go around them, but I need to speak with her, so I not-so-patiently wait until she's free and it's my turn. Of course, she instantly busies herself stirring the foods in each of the bowls, so she won't have to acknowledge me.

"Where'd your friend take off to?"

Her irritated gaze meets mine. "Why do you care?" She's straight to the point, as always. One thing I admire about her. Nothing scares or intimidates her, and if it does, she hides it well like her father.

"Just curious, haven't seen her around in a whole minute. Wanted to catch up." And reacquaint myself with her body while I'm at it.

"You wanted to sleep with her again, you mean?" She damn well knows that isn't her business. My personal life is no concern of hers, but I let her get away with it since it's her best friend and all. I need to play nice if I want her to give me the information I'm looking for.

"Of course I do. Still, haven't forgotten that sweet pussy sitting between those thighs. But no, I wanted to actually find out what all she's been up to."

"Hmph," she snorts and rolls her eyes. She's lucky I'm a decent man. Back in the day; she'd get put in her place quick.

"Where is she?" I'm done with the pleasantries. I asked her a fucking question, and if I have to talk to her ol' man about her mouth, I will.

She's quiet a minute, being stubborn, but eventually, caves with a deep sigh. "She went to my house."

"Oh, yeah?"

"Yeah, but she wasn't feeling well. With the heat, the alcohol made her sick. She was going to rest up." She follows her confession quickly. Obviously, B wanted some space if Princess is going to lengths explaining, to make sure I don't head to her place searching out Bethany.

"That's shitty."

"She'll be around once she's feeling better."

"Hope so, hate to have to disturb her and all, just to get some time with her."

"No need. Let her rest, please. Once Bethany's back, I'll tell her you wanted to talk to her."

I watch her closely as I reply, so she knows I'm dead serious on seeing her again. "Bet, appreciate it, I'll keep my eyes open for her then."

She nods, and as soon as I leave her be, I watch her take her cell out of her pocket. She types a text quickly and then stuffs it in her back pocket, glancing at me. I meet her eyes straight on, making her turn away immediately.

She knows I saw her type that message, and I'd bet every penny in my wallet she was warning her friend right now that I was looking for her. I just can't figure out why she'd need to. I thought Bethany and I left things on good terms. One day she was in my room letting me fuck her like a madman and the next she was gone. If anyone's upset, it should be me. She left me high and dry, not so much as a 'fuck you, I'm moving.' Nothing.

Women are confusing to me; they always have been. Should I show up at Viking's house and surprise Bethany? As much as I want to, it's probably not a good idea to pop up unannounced and all. She has a kid now; I have to watch how I handle this. The caveman approach Viking used on Princess won't work for me, as much as I wish that were the case.

I can't believe she even has a kid. And that I'm still interested in her after all this time as well. Of course, I thought about her randomly over the years, but now that I've seen her, it's like I've missed her.

Did I really miss her? How is that even possible? We had a few fun times, nothing to get hung up on. I think it's the fact that she took off and then years later shows up, kid in tow and isn't instantly sprung on me like she was in the past. It's fucking with my head.

"You good?" Exterminator mutters as I post up next to him and survey the people spread out around the compound. All these people here and I'd bet Princess is nice to every damn one of 'em except me. Wonder if any of these fuckers hit on B?

"Fine."

"Princess?"

"Damn Ice Queen." I shrug, and he chuckles to himself.

They find it entertaining that she doesn't like me. I'm starting to wonder if her little friend has anything to do with that and what the hell Bethany would say to turn Princess against me.

I mean, I never called the bitch after we were together, not like I could anyhow. I didn't have her number. I could've asked Princess for it, but I don't like people in my shit, and I was attacked by a lion right after that for fuck's sake. I'm pretty sure lion attack pulls the trump card in anything.

Clearly, I had my own shit to deal with. Bethany would've ended up hating me if she would've stuck around here anyhow. I was so damn angry after my attack happened, I couldn't be near a woman anyhow. Not just because I was miserable, but I wouldn't have let her see me so fucking weak and hurt.

Nobody witnessed my struggle—not a single fucking person from this club. No one knew I went to specialists or spent hours upon hours in physical therapy, choking down orders from some dumb preppy fuck griping at me to 'keep going.' Christ, I wanted to kick his goddamn teeth in, but I didn't. Preppy fuck still has every gleaming white tooth, probably thanks to some rich parents.

It was all so I could get my leg to be in the best condition it could be and ride again. There was no way in hell I was giving up riding for the rest of my life like the doctors wanted. Fuck them and fuck that lion. I overcame the struggle just like I knew I would.

I'm good now, I think. I've had years to heal and calm my anger. Now, it's time I find me a good woman to settle down with. Bethany just doesn't realize it yet, that it's gonna be her I choose. She'll figure it out soon enough, and just like riding, I'll get what I want.

I won't stop until I do.

Sapphire Knight

CHAPTER 6

"I don't believe in magic."

The young boy said.

The old man smiled.

"You will, when you see her."

- Atticus

BETHANY

Glancing at my phone, I read the text again for the fifth time since I've woken up. My dreams sucked, but I survived as usual. Maybe one day I'll be able to push the memories so far down that they'll stop finding me each time I dare to close my eyes.

When you're abused by someone who you love and is supposed to love and care for you in return, well, it screws you up inside. I'll never be like everyone else—normal. Probably why Nightmare draws me in so easily; his darkness soothes my own in a sense.

Princess messaged me while Maverick and I were taking a nap. Her text said that Nightmare was asking about me, wondering if I'd be back to the barbecue. She said he's waiting.

Should I go back? Why does he even care? I can't stop thinking of how it felt when he touched me. His presence is so large, it's impossible not to feel him on absolutely every part of my body.

The doorbell rings and I jump—startled a bit—secretly hoping it's Night, but dreading it in the same breath. If it's him, I'll most likely shit my pants, being alone with him and our son. *Shit, I've dug myself a deep hole.*

Checking the peephole, I find London on the other side and let loose the breath I'd been holding.

Opening it with a smile, I greet her with a "Hi," and gaze at her curiously.

"Hey, chica. I asked Princess where you ran off to, and when she said you weren't feeling well, I wanted to stop over to check on you."

"Oh, wow. That's nice of you, thanks."

"I know what it's like to have a little one and feel like ass. Can I get you anything or help out?"

I let her in and shut the door quickly, like Nightmare's hiding out in the bushes or something. I know he's not, but seeing him earlier has me semi-paranoid.

I don't really know what to say. Part of me wants to throw my arms around her and hug her. There've been many times, I've been sick and had to carry a trash bin around with me in case I randomly had to puke while trying to take care of a baby on my own. It was hard and every minute sucked, but I gritted and cried and puked my way through it. I never let anyone know it either, not even Princess. She would've been knocking down my door to help me, but I had to prove to myself that I could do it on my own. So far I have.

"No. I appreciate it more than you know. I think it was just the heat that got to me. I don't spend a lot of time outside anymore, and it wore me out quick."

"I know how that is. If it's not spring or fall, I don't attempt to be outside unless there's a pool nearby."

"Gotta love Texas."

"I do, just not the summer heat," she says seriously, and I grin.

"Me too," I agree and decide I really do like her.

She was nice at the compound, but one thing I admire about London is she's genuine. It's hard to find that in a lot of people, especially when you first meet them. I discovered earlier she's Cain's wife. Cain belongs to Ares' club, and he's pretty wild according to Princess. He was busy grilling when I was there earlier, so I didn't get a chance to speak to him.

"So, are you feeling better now, then?"

"Yeah, I am. I knocked out with Mav and got to recharge a bit."

"Awesome. You heading back to the festivities?"

"I should. I'm supposed to be here supporting Princess. So far, I haven't done a great job of it, either."

"Want to walk back with me then?"

"You walked?"

"Hell yeah, my mom's coming to get my kids later. I'm having some delicious drinks tonight, namely anything with tequila in it."

"Nice." Grabbing Maverick's bag, I shuffle through it to make sure we have everything already.

His toys and pack of cheese crackers are there, along with a twenty dollar bill. I doubt we'd need any money, but I stuck it in there earlier just in case. I've learned the hard way that being unprepared sucks, big time.

"Let me go check on him and see if he's fully awake."

"Okay." She nods, and I make my way to the guest room.

Maverick was awake earlier, but he was still in sleepy mode, plucking at his stuffed giraffe's hair. It's his routine until he fully wakes up and goes from zero to fifty with energy.

"Hey buddy, are you awake yet?"

"Hmmm?" he grumbles, turning toward me. He's definitely Nightmare's son; he can be so grouchy if you don't let him have 'his time.' Same as in the mornings, too, when he needs cereal, cartoons, and quiet. Just like I need coffee to function and get myself going.

Shit, maybe it's me he's like and not Nightmare.

"Do you want to go back to Prissy's barbecue and play with the other kids?" His pediatrician told me to speak to him in full sentences as much as possible. It's supposed to help with his vocabulary development.

"Ummm...yep." He sits up, already more awake than two seconds ago. I'm glad he'll have someone to play with again because he's about to be bouncing off the walls.

"Okay, I got our stuff ready. You go to the bathroom and then we'll go back. Make sure you wash your hands."

"'Tay', Momma," he replies and I go out to wait with London.

"He's coming, just having him use the restroom."

"I get it; I'm a boy's mom too. Mine's just a bit older now. He's off doing man shit and fishing with my brother. I've learned that girls are fun but dramatic."

I'm laughing when my own little man makes his way into the living room, and we take off for the compound again.

I'm about to crack open a new beer when a large hand takes it from me, opens the top, and hands the cold beverage back.

"Thank you, I could've opened it though."

He shrugs. "What kind of man would I be if I let you open it?"

"Let me?" I mock, and Ruger grins devilishly, his eyes skimming over me from top to bottom.

"You've gotten hotter."

"Well thanks, I think." Laughing, I take a good-sized gulp of the beer. I need it after earlier. "I honestly didn't think you'd remember me."

"Of course, I do, and I'm not the only one either." His eyebrows go up, and he flicks his gaze to the side.

Mine follow along and meet an irritated Nightmare's dark glare. *Well, shit.* "He's still charming, I see."

He snorts, smiling widely. "Brother or not, that's not the word I'd use for him."

"Come on, Ruger, you know you follow his lead." I giggle, and he laughs with me.

"You're gonna get me in trouble smiling like that, B, with him watching us. You know he still hasn't forgiven me for going swimming with you guys. I've gotta stay hands off when it comes to you."

"What? That was years ago!"

"I know." He shakes his head. "Still, he had his eye on you, and I should've known better. Just like Viking with Princess."

"We're nowhere near that level and never were. And I'm single, by the way, so he has no right whatsoever to be pissed at you for making me smile or being over here talking with me."

He snorts again. "Yeah, that's what you think, sweetie. I just wanted to say what's up, but I better go find someone to hit on before my brother decides he wants to beat my ass to show off in front of you. I happen to like this nose much better when it's not broken."

"You're just a flirt, no harm done. It was good seeing you, Ruger."

"You too." He winks, flashes a quick look at Night again, and takes off toward another chick like his ass is on fire.

That was weird, but I brush it off. Nightmare rarely said two words to me in front of his brothers back then. I don't know what Ruger's talking about, but I'm not going to argue with him. If he says Nightmare was territorial, then I'll take his word for it. Clearly, I never received that memo.

The sun's beginning to set, so I shuffle Maverick closer. I don't want to lose sight of him in the dark. I'd freak out. There's so much land around here, and God forbid he finds the pigs by himself. He'd try to touch them and end up hurt. I'd never forgive myself for it.

Princess told me earlier that we could take Mav to go feed them, but I don't want him out there at nighttime. Maybe I'll surprise him, and we'll walk over there tomorrow. My son seems to be infatuated with monster trucks and farm animals. I don't know if it's an age thing or what, but those two things garner his attention if he notices them.

Princess comes over to my spot with two plates of strawberry pie. My guess is she made them yesterday before we arrived. Her mom had an amazing recipe she'd use when we were teenagers. "Hey, would you keep an eye on little man for a few so I can visit the ladies room?"

"Of course, take your time." She smiles, and I know she's going to let him eat his weight in pie while I'm gone.

"Save me some." I point accusingly.

"I make no promises."

Shaking my head, I go inside to take care of business and should've guessed that Nightmare would be there for me once I finished. P said he was waiting; I should've taken her seriously. I figured he was just speaking to her, being nosey.

A strong arm wraps around me from behind, pulling me into a hard body. His warm breath hits my neck as his nose lightly brushes over my ear. He smells just like he used to—enrapturing.

"You need to let me go." *And right this minute.* Not only does he feel good, but it's more difficult for me to protest with him touching me.

"Why should I?" His deep voice grumbles, coating my skin in heat and my stomach flutters like I'm on a roller coaster. He's always done this to me whenever he was near, made me feel as if I were falling.

"I have to get back outside."

"You should just relax and come spend some time with me."

"I don't need to be anywhere near you, and you have to stop touching me, Nightmare."

"Mmm, I love it when you say my name. Now let me make you scream it."

Daydream

My breath catches, every nerve in my body waiting, practically salivating at feeling him. "Not happening."

"You never objected before." His teeth bite into the soft spot where my neck and shoulder meet. Goose bumps flood my body. I want to grind my ass against him and make him pant, but I don't. "I can make you tremble with need, make you crumble to pieces in my hands. Fuck, I missed your taste."

I never should've worn this dress.

"I'm protesting now."

"Naw, you just need a little coaxing. I can work it out." His other hand finds my thigh, smoothing up my skirt toward my center. "Remember the last time I touched you like this?"

"How could I forget?"

"Exactly. I had my fingers inside you in front of an entire bar and damn did you come hard. I can make it happen again. I can sink them knuckle deep right now."

"So generous of you."

"I missed that smart little mouth of yours, too. Close your eyes and remember how I made you shake, dollface."

The heat from his palm has my eyes slamming closed. Briefly, but it's enough to stir up the memories from the first night he ever touched me.

Three years ago...

I'm standing on the opposite side of the pool table, downing tequila and waiting for Princess to take her shot. The bar's a total shit hole, but fuck, it has some sexy-ass bikers. The huge biker she'd been tormenting outside, comes storming toward her.

He looks pissed, so I attempt to warn her, "Princess!" I call, but the music and patrons are too noisy for her to hear me, and my voice drowns out amongst the chaos.

In seconds, he's slamming her face down on the pool table and ripping her skirt up. I can't believe what I'm freaking seeing.

Oh shit, oh shit, oh shit. This isn't happening.

I stand still, shocked at first. Nobody does shit to help, so I take off for them. I have to help her!

I'm halfway around the pool table when an arm wraps around my middle. It's strong like a vice and pulls me into a body that's harder than any other I've ever been against. He even smells strong and manly, like smoke and whiskey. It's the type of smell from someone you're sure you don't want to fuck with.

"Shhh, little daydream, leave them be." It's rasped into my hair, but loud enough for me to hear him clearly. I begin to stir and pull away from the mountain of a man, but he's way too strong, easily subduing me.

He tugs me backward with him until I'm planted directly on his lap beside one of the small round bar tables. His boots part my feet, his knees and thick thighs, easily opening my legs wide for him. I can feel his hardness against my ass, and any other time I'd want to rub all over him, but I'm too distracted right now. My best friend needs me.

"I need to help her." I attempt to squirm from his hold again, but it's no use. His other hand lands on my thigh, the size making me feel dainty with him wrapped around me like this, practically consuming me.

The arm around my stomach brushes the underside of my breasts causing the peaks to stiffen almost immediately. I was an idiot thinking I'd show off and not wear a bra with a shirt cut right underneath my tits. Young and dumb comes to mind, in a biker bar no less.

"No, you need to let them handle it. You can't go startin' shit. He's claiming her, that's gonna be his ol' lady."

"His ol' lady?"

"Yeah, watch them. He's fucking her, and she's loving it."

She really is. I know my best friend, and she's enjoying every second of it. If I'm honest, it's so damn hot too. She's absolutely gorgeous with her cheeks flushed and her hair wild.

His hand trails up my thigh until it reaches my cutoff jeans. The shorts are so tiny, there's practically no barrier to keep him from touching me. "Fuck, dollface, this pussy's just waiting for me?" he growls against my throat.

I swallow and nod, becoming more and more turned on as I relax and listen to his voice. He adjusts, his cock thick and hard—ready. I know he wants me, and it spurs me on to wiggle on him just enough to make him groan.

His mouth lands on my neck, sucking and biting just as his fingers find my swollen lips. The tequila and Percocet I took earlier is thrumming through my body, heightening my pleasure. There are people everywhere, but they're all watching Princess and Viking go at it in the middle of the bar. No one's paying any attention to Nightmare and me.

"Jesus, you're wet," he mutters against my skin, and my nipples tingle, aching for his attention as well. He's the sexiest man I've ever seen—swear to God. Mix his voice with the narcotics, and it's a potent aphrodisiac on my body.

His fingers part me, rubbing my wetness before pushing inside my core. I'm still wet from making myself come moments ago outside when we went to go smoke. His movements are making me drip down the side of my thigh. Probably getting all over his jeans, too, but I don't care. I want to leave a reminder behind; I want him to remember how I felt sitting on his lap tonight.

"Ride my fingers, baby; let me feel that sweet pussy." He pumps them in me over and over while we watch Princess and Viking fuck like animals. His arm holding me tightly t him has my body going crazy at being controlled so effortlessly on his part, and in minutes, I'm coming again, all over his knuckles.

Daydream

"That's it. I feel your little cunt gripping my fingers; take what you need, baby. Let me make you feel good."

Moans escape me; it's so loud around us that I don't hold back at all. I'm sure some people have noticed what we're up to, but no one will dare say a word to the enormous biker bracing me to him. After the tremors subside and my body relaxes, his grip loosens.

I have to see him. I want him to notice my own flushed face. I want my wetness all over his lap. I've craved this man since the first time I saw him, and he's going to know it. He's that quiet bad boy you notice across the room and then dream about nearly every night for the rest of your boring life.

Twisting around, I climb over him to straddle his lap. My center rests on his hardness, and I reward him by grinding my hips in a circular motion. He made me come; now it's his turn.

"Fuck, that's good," he groans, one hand holding my ass so my pussy remains pushed up against his cock. The other lifts my shirt just enough for him to see my bare tits. His head falls forward, drawing a nipple in his mouth and grazing his scruffy beard between them. It feels absolutely fucking divine and has me picturing that beard between my thighs next.

"So good," he grumbles and sucks the wetness from his fingers, still nuzzling.

My mouth meets his right after, my tongue swirling with his, copying the motions my hips make on his lap. The kiss is short, but sinful and sweet all mixed as one.

"Pussy taste sweet?" I ask as I pull back and whisper it against his lips.

"Hell yeah." He's so close I can taste his breath mixing with my own.

"Now you know how both our pussy's taste." His gaze is confused until I tilt my head toward Princess.

"Her?" He stops, his mouth staying open as his mind races. His gaze is blistering as he stares me down, waiting to tell him that I'm kidding. I'm not.

"I was licking hers outside."

"Jesus fucking Christ." His eyes flair as he immediately stands. He grabs my arm tightly and yanks me along with him outside. "She's not the only one getting fucked tonight, dollface," he growls.

I blink, coming back to the present.

"That was such a good night, baby," he whispers, his tongue finding my neck as his palm rubs my core over my panties. He knows I love being kissed there; at least he did when we were together those nights.

Not only was it a good night, it was the night I got pregnant.

That thought has me pushing away from him. I'm panting and turned on, but thinking about my pregnancy is like a bucket of cold water when it comes to Nightmare.

"I have to go," I utter, my mind fighting against my body and take off back down the hallway. I'm almost outside when I hear him call after me. His voice has my steps faltering to listen.

It's deadly serious as he grits, "You can run, Bethany, but make no mistake, I'm a hunter. I always catch my prey. When I catch that pussy again, I'll lick it, eat it, and fuck it. Hell, I may even keep it. Be ready, baby."

I push through the screen door, and it slamming behind me loudly as I nearly run back to my best friend and son. The son he doesn't have a clue exists.

Sapphire Knight

CHAPTER 7

Nyctophilia- (n.)
Love of darkness or night,
finding relaxation or comfort
in the darkness.

NIGHTMARE

I didn't see Bethany at all yesterday. One full day of being away from her, and I haven't stopped thinking of her. It's like she crawled inside my mind, planted her ass down, and hasn't gone anywhere since. It's fucking with me.

I'm beginning to think she took my threat serious from the barbecue the other night. That's good; I wanted her, too, because it was the truth. The chase only makes me want to have her again even more. Christ, that bitch looked so fucking beautiful when I touched her, too. Jesus, took my breath away.

She's foolish if she believes I'll let her hide out the entire week she's visiting, though. I'll show up at Viking's house if I have too; I'm not above finding her. I'm trying not to be too pushy since she has a kid and all, but I won't stand completely to the side either.

"You good, brother?" Viking questions me as he stares from across the table. I sorta just zoned out in front of everyone during church. We all do it, so I shrug it off.

"I'm straight. A little distracted or whatever, but it's all good."

"He needs some pussy; his mind's too busy." Ruger snickers, and I glare in return.

I saw his dumb ass flirting with B the other night. I should make him taste his teeth for that shit. He knows we fucked before. He should also know she's off limits. He wanted her back then, and I told him to take a damn hike. Besides, he's still a Nomad, so ride off into the sunset, motherfucker.

I don't care about much, especially when it comes to the club. They do their thing, and I'm there with my support. The brothers rarely see me showing interest in any of the females around. If I like a bitch, they should back the fuck up and find another.

"It's not too busy to know you need to mind your own."

"Oh, I am brother; I assure you. I have no curiosity in her this time around. You made yourself clear the last time."

The brothers sitting around the table all watch us curiously. This isn't typical club business, but Ruger's decided to air my laundry in front of everyone apparently. *Stupid ass.*

"Good." I shut him out, not about to let everyone see me worked up. I'm glad the fucker learned quickly, though. No more going swimming and trying to hit it. That shit won't fly this time. No one's touching that pussy but me; I'll make sure of it.

Odin clears his throat. "You know she's leaving in a few days, right?"

Jesus fucking Christ. I can't believe we're discussing this shit in the middle of church right now. They all need to mind their own damn business instead of being knee deep in my shit.

"Thanks for that, Sherlock. Now can everyone mind their fuckin' business or should we go about holding hands next? Maybe watch each other take a piss?"

Blaze grins and Scot chuckles. Viking just rolls his eyes and waits for us to be quiet so he can get back to his discussion. Odin shuts up immediately; he is after all the lowest on the totem pole besides the prospects. Sure, he'll be VP someday, but he's gotta earn that shit in his brother's eyes.

Torch is like me—quiet and sticks close to Viking. Hell, we all stay close to our Prez. Who knew the craziest fucker in our group would end up being an amazing leader.

"Now, back to the women we have working for us. Does the bar still have enough security? I don't want deputy douchebag showing up and catching them whoring out the back building."

"Aye," Scot confirms. "Makin' good bit of cash too."

"No issues at all? Blaze, you've been over there a lot. Anything?"

"Nope, the whores have been staying clean, and the johns have been leaving satisfied. They're getting repeat customers and no one's beating them up any more like when they were on their own. It's going smooth as silk, Prez."

"Good. Keep them safe and clean. If anyone wants to leave, make sure they have a way too. We get a decent cut, but overall, they work for themselves, and I want to keep it that way."

The brothers nod. We've never been the type to be running pussy, but it's worked out well for everyone involved so far. The crime in Austin against the whores was skyrocketing. Women were ending up dead or nearly beaten to death, some from overdose and not making it to the hospital in time.

Since they came to us asking for help, they've had no issues, and we've gotten a healthy profit from it. I'll admit, it's nice having another form of steady cash coming in rather than lump sums from random runs. When we have brothers visiting, they can have some company if they choose to.

I haven't touched any of them either. I won't— ever. A few of them are sweet and talk to me, try to catch my eye, but it never works. I don't care about them being around the club and fucking the guys or whatever, but I prefer not to shit where I eat. I can only imagine the drama when someone gets feelings or whatever. No thank you. No easy pussy is worth that trouble.

"How was the gig?" Vike turns to me again.

"No issues." I shrug.

"Bet and Exterminator?"

"Ex and Chaos handled the drug swap while I played and kept watch."

"That's what's up. Good looking out." He takes a swig of whiskey and turns to Chaos. "Did the Mexican offer anything besides weed again?"

We've been attempting to heal the rift we have with the Mexican cartel, even though I fucking hate the thought. It's all in hopes to flush out the leader and start taking out bits of the organization. If any type of mob's around, we want it to be the Russians. We've worked well with them for years now.

"Nope, we made ourselves clear we don't want anything besides moving some green."

"No coke?"

"No, Prez. We told him we'd light his ass on fire if he brought it to us again."

"Good. Twist from the other crew handles that shit, and I don't want us dipping into their shit cause some Mexican's gettin' greedy."

"We won't cause any shit with Ares' club; you know this," I grumble, and Viking nods, sighing.

He's stressed. I'm guessing over the wedding. He's supposed to leave for a few days, too, and he's not used to taking time off. If he leaves, it's 'cause we have a run or some other reason. This time he's supposed to take a few days and do absolutely nothing with his ol' lady. My money's on them staying here. They'll post up in the house going at it nonstop, but he won't stray far from his club.

"Anything else?" He glances around, and we shake our heads. He slams the gavel, and we shuffle out the decent-sized chapel room he had built specifically for church.

"You need to get her alone with a few drinks in her system. Have the old Bethany come out and play," Ruger suggests, walking behind me. *Nosey bastard.*

"How am I supposed to do that?" I mutter. She has a kid now; I can't get her toasted with a little one to take care of. I'm a dick, but not that sort of a dick.

"I can help with that." Odin comes up beside me. I swear it seems like Viking's younger brother grows half an inch each week.

"How?"

"I'll offer to babysit so she can come to the party with Princess tonight. She was planning to stay at the house and watch movies, but if I offer to babysit, she'll come."

"Why would she let you?" I stare at him skeptically. It's a longshot, but it could work if we get Princess on board to talk Bethany into it.

"Bethany trusts me. I've seen her over the past few years. You haven't, and Maverick likes me anyhow."

"Maverick?" I ask. Cool-ass name for a kid. I shouldn't expect anything less from B, though.

"Yeah, that's her son's name. He's almost three."

"Right." I nod, but I really have no fucking clue. Why does finding this out, make me feel like an ass for not already knowing? Maybe because she's here alone, without a man and I know if it were my kid, I'd be posted up beside them nonstop. "You're sure you don't mind?"

"Yep."

"Why would you do this for me?" I'm blunt, but Odin owes me nothing, and he's young. I remember being his age, babysitting was the furthest thing from my mind.

"Because you're my brother. I have your back, and one day, I'll need you to have mine."

Ah, the fucker's smart. He knows that one day we'll all be voting on him being Vice President. He's already chalking up favors from us. He's no doubt Viking's blood. He'll make one hell of a leader someday like his brother.

"All right, Odin. You do me a solid, and I'll owe you one."

"I'm counting on it." He smirks, heading for the parking lot.

"Spider?" I turn to the shorter, dark-haired brother.

"Yeah?"

"Can you figure out where it is exactly that she lives? I need to know how far this commute is gonna be if I'm getting serious an' all."

"Of course. I can get her plate number from the security tape and run it through the DMV system. As long as her registration's up to date, her address should be current in their program. But why are you going to this trouble? It's been years since you were with her."

"I know that. Maybe it took a few years for me to realize what's important in life."

"And what about her son?"

"He fits in those plans."

Especially since I can't have my own kids.

"Okay then, give me about an hour to search the feed and get her license plate number. I'll get you an address and phone number."

"Appreciate it," I reply, and Spider's off toward his room. It's like a tech center in there with five computer monitors and a few laptops. He's got all kinds of shit going on all the time. He helps watch the club security footage when he's not out riding with Ex and them. He does pretty much anything else we need him to tech wise as well. I'd describe him as an outlaw nerd. He won't blink to bury a body and can hack into pretty much anything.

It's convenient having him around when he's here, but I try not to ever bother him for any of that stuff. Makes times like now come in handy because he doesn't even blink, offering to help out.

With Odin watching her kid, there's no reason for her not to come out to the clubhouse tonight. Her one excuse is taken care of, and Princess will want her best friend there celebrating with her.

Now I just have to figure out how to get her to talk to me. I've done a shit job of it so far. She's been avoiding me as if I have the fucking plague or some shit. Why do chicks have to be so complicated?

"You think me goin' after Bethany is pointless?" I ask my brother once he finally walks out.

"Not if you want her. Just keep in mind, it's not only B anymore. I don't want my ol' lady up my ass cause her best friend's hurt by my brother. Shit won't be fun for me or you."

"I got you; I won't mix my pussy in the club's business. Shit goes south, I'll make sure it's not her caught in the cross fire."

"Don't know how you'll manage that one, but glad you're at least considering it could happen."

"I need her to come tonight to the party. She's gotta chill the fuck out at some point so I can get her to talk to me."

"I can't believe we're having this fuckin' conversation. Last time the bitch was all over you like she was in heat or something. You just glared at her, and she couldn't get enough. What's the issue this time around?"

"Fuck if I know. Maybe because I'm not ignoring her this time? It's fucking with my head though. It's like she had my cock before and doesn't want it again. Trust me, she loved my shit, ain't no way she can deny it."

He chuckles. Viking flashing his teeth tells me that he's thoroughly amused with me tripping out over this. Fucker never does it unless we're lit off some whiskey and weed so he must be loving this a little too much.

99

"You sayin' I'm gonna have to drag her ass here tonight so you can have a shot? Just show up at the house and make her come with you."

"I can't do that in front of the kid. It may traumatize him or something."

He snorts, glancing heavenward. "You're turnin' into a pussy. That's why she's not after you, she can probably sense it. Chicks are smart, she thinks you're a pussy, she won't want your dick man."

"I am the fuck not. Just trying to think of not messing her kid up is all. Trying to be considerate; females love that shit."

"How would you know that? Since when do you make it a habit to notice women's feelings?"

"I read it somewhere, and I am now; that's all that matters."

"If you say so, brother. You want my advice? You see her tonight, pick her ass up and carry her to your room. Show her you're still a man. Tie the bitch up; fuck her until she can't walk, then be all sweet and shit. My ol' lady loves it like that."

"Princess gets her here tonight, and I'll take care of it."

"Just lock it down, brother. A good dickin' and she'll be all over you like white on rice. Hell, you may not want it after you hit it again anyhow. Could be you forgot what it was the last time."

"It was good, trust me."

"Then lock it the fuck down."

I nod, tossing back the shot of whiskey sitting on the bar waiting for me. I'm going to need about ten of them to make her feelings become invalid to me enough that if she fights me, I won't give two shits. Viking's right; I need to take care of business and remind her who's in control here. She came back, and I want her. She was mine back then, and she'll be mine again—this time for good. Once she comes to her senses, I'll move them back down here, and we can get settled together.

I can't believe after all the years out soul-searching, I'm ready to put down some roots. She's a good woman, though, just wild enough to keep me on my toes. At least she used to be. I have a feeling if she gets a taste of that again, she'll want more.

Now I'm around more and not into as much dangerous shit. Before we had our hands in dirty business, and it was a liability to care about anyone, a weakness. I wouldn't want a woman tortured or killed so enemies could get to me. They did it to Princess and Viking was a goddamn wreck. He never let anyone know it, but the man was about to completely lose it. Not sure I'd be as strong in his situation. I'd be liable to go in, guns blazing, and murder the whole lot of them if they ever threatened my ol' lady.

CHAPTER 8

Carpe Omnia

- Seize Everything

BETHANY

"I hope they'll be okay," I repeat myself for the tenth time.

Of course, I've left Maverick with a babysitter before, but this isn't the same. Odin doesn't babysit regularly, and I'm just slightly worried he'll do something out of the norm.

There's a decent-sized chance we'll come back later, and my son will be covered head to toe in fake tattoos. Generally, it wouldn't concern me, but in two days when Princess says, "I do," I don't want my kid looking like a hellion in any of her photos. Although he'd fit in with the men around him, and maybe he'll blend in more that way.

"They're right over the field at the house if they need anything. I'm sure they won't, though. This is good practice for Odin anyhow. The club sluts follow him around like lost puppies. He needs to see what happens if you're not careful."

"Thanks." I wince.

I wasn't careful; I was too trusting and ended up a single mom because of it.

"I didn't mean it like that. You were older—in your twenties—when you got pregnant. He's only eighteen and thinks he's untouchable by anything. I don't want a surprise to land him on his ass, at least not until he's older. You had a chance to be free and crazy, he's just getting to that point."

"I know what you meant. Really, it's fine. I was older but still living with my mom working a crap job. Things could've been easier. I hope Odin gets a chance to live his life some before facing the challenges I did."

"Me too, B. I won't let him be some shitty father, bailing on the back of his bike, either. I promise you that whichever woman he ends up with, he'll do right by them."

My smile's a bit shaky as I ponder over her words. She's turning into her mom, and she's so lucky for that. So are the rest of the guys; Mona was good to everyone.

It's also shaky because she still believes that Nightmare left me out to dry. I mean, he did in a way, telling me he didn't want kids and couldn't have them. He said it himself. *What kind of father would he be and why would he want that anyhow.*

Every time I begin to feel guilty or question my decisions, I have to remind myself of his words. He didn't want me; he didn't want Maverick. Nightmare didn't want us. I would've given him everything I had, too. It wasn't much, but I would've worshiped him with every beat of my heart. Too bad I wasn't enough for him.

"Enough seriousness. You have a free pass tonight. You know what that means, right?" She pulls me to her in a side hug, grin full of mischief.

"Free pass? Hardly. I still have to function tomorrow." Grinning, she rolls her eyes.

"Tonight, we have fun, Bethany. Suck it up and hold on sweet pea, it's goin' down."

"Oh, God. Why do I feel like we'll regret this tomorrow?"

"Let's not think of that now. You're trying that apple pie moonshine I told you about. That stuff is freaking amazing."

"All right, bartender, pour me one ... but only one. No puking tonight."

She laughs and leads the way into the clubhouse, straight toward the bar. She's full of trouble, and everyone always thought I was the bad one growing up. She was just as guilty as I was at getting us into something we weren't supposed to be in.

First time we drank? *Her fault.* Yep, she opened her mom's brandy cabinet and made us vodka and orange juice. It was disgusting, and we spilled it everywhere. Her mom had to know half the bottle of vodka was really water. She never said a word about it, but she didn't need too. Princess and I were so paranoid that Mona knew, we didn't enjoy it one bit. I think we walked around with our eyes wide and hands shaking for an entire month, waiting for her mom to lynch our asses.

Part of me wonders how we even survived as teens, being linked to a notorious biker club and her brother being Mr. Super Popular in school. Girls hated us for being close to him, and weird men watched us all the time. I know it was because of her father. Whether they were friend or foe, I still haven't the slightest clue.

However it happened, we made it, and now she's still trying to kill me—with moonshine. I love apple pie and doubt the liquor tastes anything like it, but if it does, I'm in trouble. You can't have too much apple pie, especially if they have whipped cream behind the bar, too. Geesh.

"Hey, Blaze? Can we each have a shot of apple pie, please?" She leans over the bar, smiling at a guy our age. His arms are covered in tattoos that look like they're on fire. So, this dude must be the cousin she's told me about. He's decent looking, but not on Nightmare's level though.

Princess filled me in how he was a total dick to her the first time they met. She said he's cool now, but for the longest, I wanted to castrate him for treating her so badly. I'm surprised Viking didn't kill him when he found out. She said he offered to and that gave him some more brownie points in my book.

106

He carefully pours us a few shots from a jar and sets them in front of us, then he takes a big swig straight from the jar for himself.

"I told you only one!" I protest over the loud music filling the small room.

Blaze grins at Princess, then at me. "No way, darlin'. You'll want another, trust me." He winks, and I understand how he's charmed her. Manners and a cute dimple with some southern twang will no doubt make your heart flutter. Mix in some moonshine, and women don't have a chance.

"Ugh." I groan, knowing I've already lost. She's got the freaking bartender on her side, so no doubt he'll feed us drinks all night as long as she bats her eyelashes at him.

"Blaze, whiskey and coke, brother." It's grumbled from behind me.

"Brother." Blaze nods and turns to make the drink.

My backside feels like it's on fire and being able to make out his grumble, I know Nightmare is close. If I guess correctly, I'd say way too close knowing him. The man has been persistent for sure and doesn't hesitate to overtake my personal space.

"You gonna say 'hi' at least, little daydream?" he mutters making my nipples harden in response. *Traitors.* The man's voice has a straight shot to my core it seems. One hand lands on my hip, and my body falters for a moment, wanting nothing more than to lean into him and rest against his strength. I want to touch him everywhere, for him to do the same to me. God, he's so good at it, like he knows all the perfect spots to hit.

"Princess," he acknowledges, playing nice.

"Nightmare," she replies, not impressed and the tension grows thicker around us. I wouldn't be surprised if P clawed his eyes out if she was given the chance to. It's my damn fault entirely, and I hate that I've created a rift between them.

"Try the shot dollface, you'll love it." His breath hits my neck, caressing the sensitive flesh, my eyelashes fluttering as it does. Thank God, he can't see my face, or he'd know I'm halfway there to giving in to him.

His drink lands on the counter in front of me as Blaze's gaze flickers over me. He's curious no doubt, why his broody brother is hovering behind me, like an overprotective bear—like I belong to him.

Prissy shoots him an annoyed look and passes me one of the rock's glasses with two fingers full of clear alcohol. "Come on, B; a toast to good friends and good times."

I tap my glass to hers, lightly bumping the bottom to the counter and then bringing it to my lips. It doesn't even smell harsh like moonshine normally does. The taste splashes over my tongue, and it's like biting into a fresh slice of cinnamon apple pie, just like she said.

I'm fucked because I instantly love it and know I'll want to drink it until I'm sick which is not good. I don't get out much—like at all—and have no alcohol tolerance anymore, so I there's no way I can hang with my bestie drinking anymore. I've turned into more of a chug-wine-before-bed or sip-a-beer-until-it's-room-temperature type.

Daydream

"Damn, that's good." I sigh, setting the empty glass in front of Blaze. Nightmare's grip tightens on my hip briefly until I wiggle away. He and alcohol don't mix—I'd end up pregnant again, and that's not happening.

"Told you." She winks, and I giggle.

I actually giggle, because I'm so happy to be here right in this moment getting to drink and relax with her. If I knew how everything was going to turn out, I would've cherished the time we had before, much more. I hate living away from her, but I didn't have a choice. I had to get away and start over. I had to go somewhere where a decent apartment was cheap to rent and where we could survive on a waitress's salary.

"Too bad Maverick's father wasn't in the picture to help you with him, or else we could do this more." She glares at Night behind me, and I choke, coughing.

"Princess!" I gasp and yank her away from the bar, away from him. "You can't say that stuff, please," I plead, the music drowning our conversation away. I can't believe she just said that next to him.

"Why not? I'm your best friend; of course, you're going to tell me what happened. Does he think he can just stand right there, touching you like he owns you, without me opening my mouth? He can't have his cake and eat it too, doesn't work that way. He wants you, he wants Maverick. There is not one without the other."

My eyes become watery. She has no idea what she's talking about. I should admit everything to her, the entire story. He doesn't know Maverick's his, and even if he did, I don't think anything would change. I seriously doubt he'd care, but I'm not wanting to feel that heartache in my soul as well.

Being shot down once from him is enough for me to remember for the rest of my life. I wish he wanted us both, but I'm not going to fool myself into believing that fairy tale can be mine. He doesn't want to be a father; I won't force him into that position.

"Please. I just want to relax and have some fun."

"What's going on?" Viking's inquisitive gaze flashes over us both as he pulls Princess to his chest. Always in protection mode when it comes to his woman. She's lucky.

"Nothing, your ol' lady's making me drink moonshine."

"Ah." He grins. "It's good."

"It's amazing!"

"Then let's have some," he finishes, pulling Princess with him to the bar. She, in return, tugs me along with her.

We each pick up the other full shots we'd left behind, and Blaze pours Viking a tumbler that's three-quarters full. The man's the size of a mammoth, so naturally, his shots are supersized too.

"Come on, brother, join us in celebrating." He includes Nightmare, and, of course, Night readily agrees, saddling up next to me as he's poured his own super-sized shot as well. At this rate, I'll be trashed within the hour.

"What we toasting too?" Night asks while staring down at me, his eyes saying so much but I'm unable to read him.

"To women we can't forget," Viking mutters, while tinking his tumbler to Princess' shot. "To women worth being better for."

She finishes, "And to men who're nothing but trouble." He sends her a curious glance but doesn't protest. Instead, downing the alcohol in two gulps and finishing by pressing his lips to hers in a scorching kiss.

I'm happy she's found the love of her life. I'm even slightly jealous of it. Not in a bad way; I just want that love for myself.

Nightmare's knuckles find my chin, tipping my head up to his, but I don't give him the chance. Turning back to Blaze, I put on a large smile. "Hey, Blaze, can I get a Sprite, please?" I need something to cool me off.

"Just a Sprite? Want me to add some vodka and cherry or anything?" I hate vodka, and even that sounds delicious. No wonder he's the bartender.

"No thanks, just the Sprite for me, please. I need something other than alcohol in my stomach or I won't be able to hang with this one for very long." I tilt my head over toward my friend who's still making out with her man. Years later and they act like two horny teenagers, never getting enough of each other.

"Hmmm, that's not what I've heard. According to the boss lady, you were quite the partier back in the day."

"Yep, I was, but I've calmed down since then. It's not fun being hungover the next day I've learned."

"Truth," he agrees, handing me the large, fizzy soda. He threw a cherry on top for me, so that was sweet.

"We had fun, and I don't remember you being so bad off that we couldn't roll around the next day." Nightmare pulls my face back toward him, and I lick my lips. My hand falls to his chest, attempting to keep some mandatory space between us. Any closer and I'll melt right here in front of him.

He leans down, brushing his nose against mine as his deep voice continues to mutter, "In fact, I remember we had a great time—fucked up, posted against the side of a bar. Remember that, dollface? You had marks all over your back from the brick." Princess' eyes grow wide as they meet mine, and the memories flash through my mind of the night he's talking about.

He'd pulled me outside the bar. Rushed and hot after I'd divulged my secret of having tasted Princess mere moments before he'd sucked my taste off his fingers. I wanted him so badly at that point I thought my body would explode if he held out.

It'd been like he was teasing me in the days before. Each time I'd seen him, he'd throw me a brief, irritated glance and nothing more. I knew he wanted to fuck me. I could feel it in the air, in the way his pissed-off gaze practically singed me each time it landed on me.

"So, I'm getting fucked too, hmmm?" I giggle, following behind as he rounds the corner of the building. I'm practically thrown up against the brick, his body coming to mine in a hurry as if he can't feel me fast enough.

Daydream

"Bet your sweet ass, you are. I'm gonna fuck you so hard, you won't be feeling anyone else there but me— ever. I'll be your goddamn Nightmare all night tonight, baby, and you'll be my daydream."

Those words coming from his mouth as he pulls my shorts free are like ice on a hot day. Just what I need to hear for my core to crave him sinking blissfully deep into me. Most men are pansies, overworking to get me to spread my legs for them. Nightmare, however, gets right to it.

"Then fuck me, Nightmare," I whisper, relenting and his eyes alight with a fiery storm. He's big and strong and hung like a goddamn horse. His cock stirring between his legs is the biggest dick I've ever seen in my life. Long and thick and needy, exactly what I want from him. He's right about me never feeling anyone else. How could I with a man like him?

"Oh my God." Gasping in delight, I take his length in my hand—my fingers not being able to touch each other, his girth is so dense.

"That's right, dollface, you won't be walking tomorrow." He winks, a roguish grin painted on his lips.

You know how many guys say that shit and then it never holds true? All of them. In this case, Nightmare is one hundred percent telling the truth, and for the first time in my life, I'm scared of a cock.

Pulling my hand free, he takes both my wrists in one of his much bigger hands. Nightmare posts them above my head, against the rough brick behind me. He wraps his other arm with muscles the size of my thighs around my waist, lifting me clear off the ground. The man clearly knows what he wants and fuck if it isn't unbelievably sexy.

113

A small moan escapes my lips at his movements. The control and no hesitation on his part has me panting to have him inside me. His cock bobs, straight up, seeking out my center. It's so fucking big, he doesn't even need his hands. He simply lowers me down on him, my pussy swallowing him up like the greedy, overly excited bitch she is.

One powerful bounce of his hips and I'm sliding down farther, his length ripping through me in the most delicious ways that I've experienced.

"Sweet baby Jesus," I groan, and he chuckles darkly. "You are one big boy."

"I didn't descend from above beautiful; I ascended from hell. Nothing good and pure could have a cock like this. And I'm all man, no boy around here," he growls and drives into me hard.

I scream loudly and love every second of the pain, of the perfection. There was a reason he was holding out on me, but no more. I may not be able to walk tomorrow, but I'll make sure he's so satisfied that he never wants another.

He may believe he's from hell, an outlaw biker who's mean and dangerous. But I don't agree with him. Nothing this perfect could come from below.

He fucks me with purpose, the rough edges of the brick scraping my back with each harsh drive. I don't know if he's proving his point to me or trying to make me praise God about him some more. His arm must be torn to shit as well from bracing me and taking the brunt of his motions.

"You gonna cry, baby?" he mutters, watching me with delight. He must be used to weak women. I may not

be too strong, but one thing I'm not is weak. And if I were, I'd never let a man like this see it. He needs a mate that can match him, and I'm determined to be that one for him.

"No, I want it harder."

His eyes widen as his eyebrows raise, surprised at my admission. "Harder?" He must not be used to hearing that request.

"Yes, harder, Nightmare. Make me feel you."

"Oh, you'll feel it all right." It's muttered darkly as his body slams into mine, the breath nearly leaving my lungs as he sinks into me fully. There's hasn't been a man like him before, and it has me spinning. He's purely sinful, everything I crave and desire, yet everything I shouldn't have, everything that's bad for me.

Nightmare calls to my dark side, I want to drink a little more, take another pill, and fuck even harder. He could be my destruction, yet it's the first time he's been this close to me—the first time I've felt him.

He bounces his hips again, thighs with thick muscles, built like some sort of Greek god. His cock drives through my core, taking its pleasure and giving me mine in return. He's so deep that his dick hits the perfect spot. One more caress and his cock has me grinding into him, seeking more.

"More, please, right there!" I call, my eyes clamping shut as the sensations begin to make me see bright colors behind my eyelids. "Ohmygod more, just fuck me, already!"

The words flip a switch; he drops my wrists, his free hand coming to my throat. One harsh squeeze, cutting off my breath has me coming, a scream fighting to break free as he pounds into me. It must be the tipping point for him too, as he stares at me full of fury, pumping into me over and over, so quickly that my head hits the brick. It hurts, but each sample of pain only heightens my pleasure he so easily supplies me with.

Gasping, my mouth falls open as dizziness starts to cloud my vision. His forehead is against mine, his mouth taking my own with a vengeance as his cock bursts inside my core. His cum is hot and thick, each splash warming my center in a blissful assault, and all I can think of is how I want more.

I want all of it, everything he'll give me. I want him.

"Fuck, you're sexy when your cheeks redden like that," Nightmare mutters, and it brings me out of the memory, of the first time he had me. The first time I had a piece of him. It was the night he possessed my body and my soul. I knew he owned me.

"Ummm," I reply, blinking quickly, trying to clear the thoughts away.

"You okay, Bethany?" Princess interrupts, garnering my attention.

"Yeah, just a little...dizzy." Sighing, I gulp some of the Sprite down.

This is why I can't drink around Nightmare. He doesn't even have to touch me; the memories alone could make me self-destruct.

CHAPTER 9

I'm a daydreamer
and a night thinker.

NIGHTMARE

My knuckles brush her flushed cheek, and her breath catches. She's so fucking beautiful. I was stupid to let her slip through my fingers the last time we were together. Each time I'm around her, I see more and more what I've been missing out on.

Had I never been attacked, I'd like to think things would've turned out differently. She was so fuckin' crazy back then, too. Just plain wild; I would've loved taming her. I doubt there would've been any dull moments between the two of us.

"Please?" she mumbles as her head turns to the side away from my touch. Almost as if it hurts her each time I do it. I don't know why she's being like this, so stubborn. I'll break through her barrier; I just need a little more time with her relaxed like this.

"Dollface?" I stare down at her, wanting to place her cheeks in my palms and own her lips.

"Just stop touching her already!" Princess interrupts, about to take a step forward when Viking catches her arm, holding her in place.

Flashing an irritated glare in his direction, one he's easily able to read, I remain quiet. He needs to keep his bitch in check. I'm getting real tired of her attitude toward me when I've done nothing but be respectful toward her since day one. She has no reason to treat me the way she does, and I've kept my mouth shut, but enough is enough.

I don't want to disrespect my Prez or his ol' lady, but if she doesn't butt the fuck out, I will say something. It'll get ugly, but me and Vike have been cool for a long time. He'll at least hear me out before he tries to break my neck.

"Cinderella," he warns gruffly at my glower and pulls her closer to him. He whispers something into her hair behind her ear that we can't hear. Whatever it is, she doesn't like it, but her trap stays closed, and, for that, I'm grateful.

"Come here, B, do a shot with me." My hand grasps the tips of her fingers to tug her toward me a little more.

"I can't." Her head shakes, her eyes sad.

"Fuck this shit." Princess steps forward, furious, not heeding Viking's warning any longer. "Here's an idea, Nightmare. Don't fucking touch her anymore! Can't you get the message? You didn't want her when she was pregnant with your kid; why the fuck should you have her now? You're a real piece of shit, you know that? All this time I've kept my mouth shut out of respect for Viking and Bethany, but I'm done. You deserve to at least get one ass chewing from us. What kind of motherfucker deserts his own kid? You shouldn't even be anywhere near her, you piece of shit! You're lucky I didn't slit your throat myself," she spits out angrily, staring me down like I'm worse than the scum on the bottom of toilet.

Her words begin to register, and my stomach turns. I feel sick like I could puke. My first thought is that it can't be true. I can't have kids; the doc told me a long time ago that my guys were slow swimmers. I guess it doesn't mean I couldn't have kids for the rest of my life, but at the time, he told me not to be too concerned about getting anyone pregnant.

But with Bethany? How did this happen and I didn't know. My kid? With her?

My eyes flash to my brother, but his are wide with shock as well. He didn't know, and that brings me a little bit of peace, knowing he didn't betray me. But Princess no doubt knew, and she took all those visits to see Bethany and *my* kid. And then B, staying away for so many years and then showing up out of the blue, and what thinking we'd forget who she was or some shit?

My eyes snap back to the woman in question. Tears drip down her cheeks, and she looks so fucking guilty. She's kept this from me this whole time. She made my son into a big dirty fucking secret and kept that secret from me, his own father.

I've never wanted to knock someone's teeth in so fucking badly in my entire life. I've never felt such fury, such deception, either. My body becomes hot, shaking taking over my limbs as I attempt to stay rooted in place.

For this right here, I could kill her. In this moment, I'd love to wrap my hands around her throat and squeeze until she takes her last breath. She took something from me. She stole from me. She stole something I can never get back. *Time.*

A roar escapes, loud enough to be heard over everything in the bar. Rage overtakes my vision as I slam my hands to the bar, swiping my arm through the glasses. They fly in all directions, glass shattering as it lands everywhere.

"You fucking bitch!" I yell—beyond pissed. How could she do this to me? I've done nothing to deserve this treatment from her. My hands clench in fists, the shaking making me feel like my body's completely losing it.

My gaze clouded, I snatch her arm, yanking her to me, with such force her mouth pops open, and her eyes widen, terrified at my outburst. "You fucking stole from me, woman. I should take your motherfuckin' life for that shit. I got a kid—a *motherfuckin'* kid—you kept

Daydream

from me? That boy you got with you, he belong to me, Bethany?"

"Ummm..." She stutters, breathing heavy, shocked.

"You should be scared, bitch. You open that fucking trap right now and you tell me if that's my kid. Don't you dare lie either; I'll cut your goddamn tongue out if you try that shit. You fuckin' feel me?"

Every eye in the bar is trained on us. I don't do this; I don't lose control—not ever and not in front of my brothers. I'm the calm one who's always pissed off but keeps to myself. They don't see me yell, and I'm usually only violent in front of Exterminator when we need to torture somebody.

And I never raise my voice at women. I saw my father do it too many times in the past that I promised myself to never be anything like him. But this woman has me angrier right now than I've ever been in my entire damn life. I've never wanted to beat the life out of someone like I do right now. I feel so hurt and betrayed it's consuming any feelings I had for her.

"Yes," she replies, her lip wobbling as tears rain down her face.

"You get the fuck back to that house and check on my son. And don't you dare think about running, 'cause I will hunt you down to the ends of the earth if I have to. Tomorrow we talk, but right now...right now you get the fuck outta my sight, so I don't do something I'll regret down the road." I release her roughly to where she stumbles back a few steps and Princess catches her.

Princess' empathetic gaze meets mine; she bites her lip and whispers, "I'm so sorry, Night; I thought you knew."

I glare at her for a moment then turn my back to her. Blaze immediately sets a glass down with a bottle of Jack beside it. Any man here knows I'm getting wasted. I have to drown out this demon trying to break free before he causes unfixable damage. If I let myself free and I end up hurting B for this, I will never forgive myself for it.

She thought I knew? How could I? And how could they believe I'd be a deadbeat father? No one has a clue about my life growing up; it's nobody's business, so they just assumed I'd be a shitty dad? Fuck that.

Yes, I'm dangerous. Yes, I'm violent. Yes, I'm an outlaw biker that was a Nomad for many years.

Not once in my lifetime have I ever hurt a woman, nor have I hurt a child or treated them wrongly. Sure I've been a dick, fucked then left, but they always knew the score. Bethany knew what it was all about from the start.

Her question that night comes back to me, the last time I saw her.

"We don't need a condom? What if I get pregnant?"

"I'm sterile and clean; I told you this the other night when we fucked."

"Right, I'm just being paranoid."

I kept kissing down her neck, sinking inside that tight cunt of hers, not thinking anything more.

Shaking my head, I take a large gulp of Jack. I'm a goddamn idiot, and she knew; she had to. After that conversation, it was like she was a ragdoll, not into it. I waved it off as her not feeling well. But she was fucking pregnant, with my kid inside her, and she never said another word about it.

Growling, I slosh more liquid in the tumbler and drain it. I hear Viking and Princess arguing behind me before he finally cuts her off.

"My brother needs me tonight. You go find her and deal with that shit," he says angrily, and the barstool beside me fills with his oversized body. No kiss or anything goodbye to his woman. Yep, he's pissed. It's shitty, but it makes me feel a touch better knowing that he was clueless and that he's angry too.

Sure, it didn't happen to him, but his ol' lady was keeping secrets again, and the last time that happened there was a huge blowout between them. I was in the room next door to them, and they like to yell when they argue. They're supposed to be getting married in two days, too, and this pops off.

Just fucking great. I hate being the source for the drama this time around. It wasn't voluntary that much is certain. I can't believe the Ice Queen knew and didn't say shit this entire time. She thought I knew? No wonder she treated me like dog shit all the time.

He signals for a cup, and Blaze grabs another tumbler. Viking pours his nearly to the top and takes a healthy swig, sighing.

"Don't know what the fuck to say, brother. I'm just gonna sit here, so you aren't alone. We don't have to say shit if you don't wanna, just know, I'm here."

I nod. I'm not a talker, but I'm so damn mad inside, I should open my mouth. If I don't get it out somehow and drown it with the alcohol, I'm liable to throw a couple bodies in a dumpster and light that shit on fire.

"Truthfully…I want to kill someone right now."

"Bet. Want to head into Austin to one of the bars? We may at least find a fight."

Draining the rest of the Jack, I turn his way. "Let's fucking do it. I need to pound something, and a low-life piece of shit may help get some of it out."

"All right then." He lets out a sharp whistle, calling everyone's attention. "Bitches need to stay back, we're gonna take care of some shit."

The club sluts look disappointed, a few wives worried, but the guys? They're up for a good fight any day of the week. Most of us have demons inside we like to expunge when we have the chance to, and tonight's definitely one of them. I need to hurt someone, to get this blackness out that's trying to take over my heart.

We all load up on our bikes, the rumble of the club rolling out together sounding more of an angry roar. No doubt they'll hear us coming, wherever we end up. May God be on their side, 'cause they're damn sure gonna need His help tonight.

BETHANY

I slept terrible last night. I couldn't stop crying, and now my face is so puffy, I look like I ate a giant marshmallow. Princess was livid. It's been a long time since I've seen her that upset over something and it was directed at me.

She feels like she's helped me betray her ol' man by keeping my secret. I hate that she thinks that. It was entirely my fault; I take full responsibility for it.

Sure, I didn't tell Viking, and neither did she, but Princess believed that she was just keeping mine and Nightmare's business private. But it was only my business since Nightmare didn't even know about it.

I can't believe it went down like that last night; what a clusterfuck. I can't be angry at my best friend for saying something; I can only be upset at myself over this whole thing. I shouldn't have kept Maverick's existence from Nightmare; but, at the time, I believed I was doing the right thing. I felt like I was protecting my son, and I would most likely do the same thing if I were to go through it again.

Night was livid; I've never seen him like that. But was he angry because I kept Maverick secret from him, or was he angry that he has a child? Or that he has a kid and didn't know about it? Is he happy about it at all?

I know he was mad, but know nothing else. I wish he'd have told me his feelings last night. We're supposed to talk today, and part of me is terrified he's going to kill me.

"He's going to kill me," I whisper it out loud, a tear dropping free, and Princess shakes her head.

She glances at Maverick sitting on the couch, watching cartoons with his bowl of cereal. "He won't. If it weren't for you being Mav's mom, though, he probably would have last night."

"You're not helping."

"I'm just keeping it real with you. He won't hurt you; he knows Maverick needs his momma."

"Everyone in the club is going to hate me now, too." Sighing, I shake my head. I don't want them to hate me.

"They won't hate you, but they probably won't say much to you either. What you did affects Nightmare, and that affects the club. They'll all wait to see how he treats you first because that's their brother."

"I should just go." My lip trembles, feeling absolutely horrible inside. I don't want to be here with everyone angry at me. My son doesn't need to see or feel that either. This trip was supposed to be fun, and I've managed to ruin it.

"No, that's the last thing you should do. Look, you ran and hid the last time, B, and that didn't work out so well for you in the end. I believe Nightmare when he says he'll hunt you down. It'll be much worse if he has to go looking for you versus you staying and facing the music."

"I can't let Maverick see him hurt me. I promised myself that my son will never experience abuse or hate. It doesn't matter if it's directed toward me; I don't want him to be around it at all."

"I told you, Nightmare won't hurt you, not like that. You should've thought about this shit when you first moved. I still don't get what you were thinking.

Protecting your baby, yes; but keeping him from his father is no good, Bethany. You really dug a deep hole."

"I know, fuck." Swiping at the tears, I attempt to pull myself together. I don't want Mav seeing me like this. He'll freak out if he witnesses me crying and will probably start crying too.

"What should I do?"

"About which part?" She hands me another tissue.

"All of it."

"You pull your big girl panties on and deal with it, babe."

"I hate panties," I grumble, and she laughs. It's the first time since before all this blew up in my face. "You think he'll want to be a dad?"

"Only one way to find out, I suppose; but if how he reacted last night is any indication, my bet would be yes." She shrugs as the rumble of bikes grow louder. "Looks like you may be finding out sooner than later."

"Oh God."

Sapphire Knight

CHAPTER 10

Carpe Diem

- Seize The Day

NIGHTMARE

I take her to IHOP because what the fuck else am I supposed to do? I'm no good at this talking thing, and we damn sure need to do a lot of it. And about everything, it appears.

"I'm surprised," she admits, sipping her coffee.

"You're surprised? Should probably be the opposite, dontcha think?"

"I mean with you bringing me here." She gestures to the restaurant. "I wasn't expecting us to go anywhere or you to let me ride on the back of your bike."

That wasn't the smartest of moves on my part. She kept her distance until I took a turn and then she was pressed up against me. I'm still too pissed at her for it to turn me on, but I still felt something tilt in my chest having her that close to me.

"I'm too angry to be alone with you. I don't trust myself yet, and the last thing I want to do is hurt you. Figured breakfast was a good place to start. We have a barrier between us." I point to the table. "As for my bike, only an important woman rides back there. You being the mother of my child, I'd say that makes you pretty fucking important."

She swallows, nodding, and I think her eyes tear up. Her gaze locks on her lap, so I can't get a good enough look to know for sure, though. I don't get why she'd be so upset if that's the case.

I'm not one to sugarcoat shit; I've made it clear in the past. Just because she wasn't honest with me, doesn't mean I'm going to stop being honest with her. I've kept it real with her since day one. I have no reason to pussyfoot around or keep shit from her besides club business. That will never be her business.

"The fuck you expect, B? You want me to just brush it off and forgive you? That's not how this is gonna work, baby. You may as well just bite the bullet and make peace with it now. Ain't happenin'."

She clears her throat, her gorgeous irises meeting mine for the first time today. "Maverick means everything to me. I thought I was doing what was best for him."

"What, having him grow up without a father? Having him believe that I'm some shitbag that doesn't want to be in his life? You're a goddamn fool if you think there's one ounce of justification or truth to either of those options."

"You told me you weren't cut out to be a father, Nightmare. You said it yourself, what would you do with a kid? What was I supposed to think? I was young, pregnant, and scared. My life was changing!"

"That's just it, you didn't fucking think. Or just maybe you would've discovered I wanted kids and still do. Maybe if you weren't so goddamn selfish, you'd have let me have a chance to explain. I'd have told you that my doc made it clear I didn't need to be too concerned with making babies. It wasn't something I thought was an option at all or I would've wrapped it up. Not saying I don't want my son, just that I would've protected you better."

"I did think, I just didn't think about you. I had to do what was best at that moment for *my* son. I'm sorry that I took the option away to be a father from you. I was under the impression you didn't want kids, period. I was just some random fuck to you, Nightmare. I wasn't stupid enough to believe you'd change your ways to be father of the year. For once in my life, I did think clearly; those thoughts just didn't include you."

Her words damn near cut me they're so sharp. At least she's finally being honest with me.

"Christ, you infuriate me. I've never wanted to snap someone's neck so fucking badly as I do yours. You get that, right? That I'm enraged by what you've done? He's my kid, B, *my kid.*"

"I'm sorry, Nightmare. I really am. If I had even an inkling of belief you wanted Maverick, I wouldn't have ever left."

"That's another thing. You fucking took off and didn't come back for years. You basically snuck off and kept my son a secret. I don't even know what to say to you about that. I will say this, though; don't ever think you can pick up and leave like that again. I meant what I said, Bethany, I will find you. I don't care if I have to search until my last dying breath, you will never hide *my son* from me again."

A tear falls down her cheek, and I'm a bastard because I enjoy the sight of it. I'm hurt inside, and I want to make her hurt in return. She kept the one thing I've always searched for, away from me—family.

Why else would I join a damn biker club? I was a Nomad to be on my own, but I always had a few brothers with me, just as fucked up as me, it seemed. I thought that life was what I'd needed all along to be happy until I started seein' brothers getting serious and having kids. It opened my eyes to more that I was missing in my life. For years now, I could've had it too.

Fucking bitch.

"I won't, I promise."

"I have a place here. We'll get you moved in after the wedding."

She snorts, and my brows rise. "We're not moving. Maverick and I have our own apartment, and I have a job that I need to show up for next week."

"Don't give a shit about any of it."

"I mean it. You can meet Maverick, but we aren't moving."

"Oh, I can meet him? How fucking generous of you."

"Can we go now, please?"

"Huh?"

"We aren't getting anywhere, and this is pretty embarrassing having the people around us overhear this conversation."

"Oh, sorry, I'm embarrassing you? Guess you shouldn't have kept my fucking kid from me then, huh?"

"You're a bastard."

"Yeah, I am. Get used to it dollface, you're stuck with me for life."

Another tear falls, and I grin. I really am a fucking bastard. Time she learns who's in charge. She'll quit her job and move down here; I'll make certain of it.

She can think that she's stubborn, but I'll be up there riding her ass and seeing my kid every weekend until she gives in. I set up roots here; Bethany and Maverick are now a part of those roots, and I need to stay close to the club, to my brothers. Hope she enjoys club life, cause it's about to become hers if I don't kill her first.

"Grab your shit. We can take off, and you can introduce me to my son."

She sighs and climbs to her feet, grabbing her phone. We head out to my bike, and I secure my helmet to her head. I only have one, and at this point in time, her life is far more precious than mine is. She's the mother of my child, and that's pretty fuckin' important.

"So, you like animals, huh?" I watch as Maverick stands on one of the two-by-fours that encase the pigpen so he can see them better. He keeps oinking and snorting at them like they'll talk back. It's pretty entertaining.

"Ummm...yep."

He waves to a pig as it walks in front of us. Maverick sounds just like his mom. I thought little kids weren't supposed to talk really well, but he does a good job. He rambles a little, and I lose track of what he's saying 'cause it's excited and fast, but everything else I've heard just fine.

He likes animals and trucks and my motorcycle. It's a trip seeing so much of myself in him, too. If I had kept my hair shorter, we'd probably look even more alike.

"I like playing the drums with my band," I admit randomly. Not too sure what to say to a kid really. I'm not around them much; well, not enough to have conversations and all. I could teach him how to play, though, if he wanted to learn. If the Flying Aces didn't only have gigs in bars, I'd have him come and watch too.

He stays quiet, so I try again. "Maverick, do you know what dads do?"

"Ummm..." He shrugs his brown gaze just like mine, flicking to me briefly before going back to the hogs.

"We teach you cool stuff like moms do; only man stuff. We're kind of like moms, but different," I try to explain but realize I suck when I hear Bethany giggle behind us. "What I mean is, I'll be here for you when you need something, like your mom."

"Momma?" Mav cocks an eyebrow, glancing at B and then back to me.

"Yep, just like her, only I'm bigger and stronger so I can protect you good."

"Snacks?"

"You're hungry?"

Bethany interrupts. "No, he wants to know if you'll get him snacks like I do."

"Oh." I blink and nod. "Yep, I'll get you snacks, too."

He grins at that, and it's like my whole world tilts with that small smile.

Snacks and animals, I can do that, no problem. First off, I need to get him a puppy, and then he'll never want to leave. Bethany has no idea what she's up against.

BETHANY

I have to keep chanting to myself not to cry. It's amazing seeing Nightmare and Maverick together like this, even if Nightmare has been anything but kind to me today. He's treated me like I'm nothing, and, sadly, I know that I deserve this from him. He should hate me, especially after seeing how happy he is with Maverick.

Now, I wish I could go back and do everything over. I'd tell him that very night I asked him about us using protection. I'd share with him that I was sick and the doctor believed I was pregnant. We'd argue that it wasn't true and then he'd learn it really was. He could see Maverick be born and hold him that very first day he came into the world. Things would be so different, life would be different, and he wouldn't detest me as he does now.

Nightmare doesn't have to hate me; I'll punish myself enough for what I've done. I thought I was protecting my son, but really I was only keeping him from someone who loves him already. These past few years could've been so much easier having Nightmare in our lives to help. Even just being there would've made an impact. I could've come to see Princess more, and the entire club could've known about Maverick this whole time.

I was so stupid. I'll never be able to forgive myself from keeping Maverick away from someone who loves him like Nightmare so easily does. One look at my son and he didn't even question it. It's easy to see looking at Mav's little face, who he belongs to. He's Nightmare's son, no doubt.

"Night?"

"Yeah?"

"Do you think you have any other kids out there that you don't know about?"

"I doubt it; I make it a habit of using protection."

"So, why was it different with me?"

He shrugs, turning away and cutting me off again. Maybe someday I can get him to answer the question, but it definitely won't be today. And Maverick damn sure gets the shrugging from him, not me.

Princess' wedding passed in a blur filled with me apologizing a million times. Not only to Night but to the few of the club members who actually spoke to me. I was nervous prior to coming, but it was nothing compared to how I felt inside knowing that everyone around us knew what I'd done.

I felt like a giant asshole, and while I was excited for Princess to tie the knot, I'm extremely happy to be back home now. I get four days of peace to myself with Mav, then Nightmare will be here visiting. To say I'm shitting a brick knowing he'll be in my home is an understatement.

What are we supposed to do while he's here? It's going to be so freaking awkward now that he hates me so much. It was weird enough seeing him before he knew we had a child together.

At least now he'll stop trying to get me to sleep with him. Not that I didn't want to; it was just...he'd hurt me. Well, I thought he did anyhow. These past few years were wasted with my stupidity, all from a misunderstanding.

I'm still trying to figure out if it's a blessing or a curse now with Night. He could make the rest of my life hell if he wanted to. All we can do is wait and see what happens, and that's the scary part.

I hope he can move on enough to forgive me one day even though he swears he never will. To witness the hurt and betrayal in his eyes when he found out crushed me inside. I thought it was terrible him hurting me back then; it was nothing to how awful I felt knowing I'd caused him so much pain inside.

Me: We're home.

Nightmare: Good. Hug Maverick for me. See you guys Friday.

Me: Okay, I will. You got the address I sent you earlier?

Nightmare: Yes.

Me: Okay.

See, not awkward at all. *Ugh.* What am I going to do? I have to figure out a way to fix this. Not make it all better, I'm not that naïve to believe that could happen overnight, but there must be something I can do to help a little.

My gaze lands on Maverick's baby picture. It's one of my favorites with him in an old-fashioned tin as a bathtub with bubbles flying all around him. Princess took us to have his pictures done when he turned one, and they came out so adorable. I'd have never been able to afford it, and she gave me one of the best gifts ever.

Nightmare missed all of it, nearly three years' worth of firsts, and he saw none of it. I can start by sharing it all with him, so I use my phone to take a picture of the photo.

Me: Maverick turns one, my favorite picture of him.

I don't get a reply, but I didn't expect one. It could help or make him angry; I'm not sure which one. I'm going to do my best to share with him everything he missed, so each day for the rest of the week, that's what I do. I pick out a picture that means something.

Day two I sent him a picture of our son drooling, showing off his first tooth. Day three I sent him a photo when Mav decided it was time to walk. Day four I sent him a picture of Maverick grinning, giving me a thumbs-up. He'd just fed a giraffe at the Cameron Park Zoo in Waco and thought it was the coolest thing ever.

Day five Nightmare shows up on our front porch, so I skip the text, surprised to see he actually came. I don't know what had me doubting him, but I shouldn't have. The first thing I notice—his hair. The dreads are gone, and he looks like the old Nightmare—*my* Nightmare that I remember. Strong and imposing and just plain beautiful.

Sapphire Knight

CHAPTER 11

Carpe Noctem

- Seize The Night

NIGHTMARE

"You're here," she squeaks. Bethany's eyes are wide as she pulls the front door to her apartment open.

"Told ya I would be." I wink and walk past her, coming inside without an invitation. "Maverick?" I call loudly since he's not right there when I first enter.

"Dad? Momma, is my dad here?" he yells. It's an excited jumble, but I still figure it out easy enough. My chest swells, hearing him call me his dad. He knew it was me, just from hearing his name.

"Yes, he's here! Come say hi," she replies toward a narrow hallway off the side of the living room.

He comes out running, going full speed, jumping when he reaches me. My knees bend, and I catch him, lifting him until he nearly touches the ceiling. In one week, he's become my entire world.

"Yow're here, for weal."

"I am." Nodding, I grin. I can't stop the smile overtaking my mouth at getting to see him again. I'm overjoyed by hearing him talk and visiting with him. "When I promise you something, Maverick, it'll always happen, you can count on it. I don't break promises. Got it?"

He nods, and we fist bump as I easily balance him in my grip with one arm.

"Missed you, little dude."

"Missed yow." He smiles, and I set him back down, turning to find Bethany watching us wistfully.

Setting my backpack down, I glance around the small space. "Where am I staying?"

"Wif me," my son instantly answers, and I chuckle.

"Hey buddy, your bed's a little too small for Daddy. His feet would fall off." B laughs.

Maverick's finger goes to his temple and he taps it a few times, clearly thinking it over. "Ummm..." He shrugs, and she laughs again.

"You can sleep on the couch. We don't have a spare room."

"Him will fit in yowr bed, Momma."

She swallows roughly and shoots an uneasy smile at me. "We'll figure it out, Mav; don't worry." Her gaze meets mine. "Have you eaten?"

"Nope."

"Well then, guess we can start there," she replies, and I'm not sure it's for me or her. I think she's reassuring herself.

"You don't have a gig this weekend?"

"Nope, bar's got another band visiting."

"I'll get some food started."

The day flies by hanging out with the kid, and it's not until the next night that I'm really drawn to Bethany.

Turning over on the uncomfortable couch, I steady my breathing to listen.

"No!" B grounds out, and the sound carries out my way from her room. The living room is in the middle, separating hers and Maverick's rooms. I doubt he can hear his mom, but I definitely can.

On alert, I grab the blade from my pants that I'd discarded beside the couch earlier and quietly creep toward her hall. Her door's cracked open, in case our son needs her in the middle of the night. I use it to my advantage, following the wall so I can be hidden by the partially-closed door.

"No, please?" she groans, sorrow and fear coating her voice.

She sounds as if she's being tortured, and no amount of anger I had from her secrets can keep me from wanting to protect her, to save her from whoever's hurting her in there. It's in this moment that I realize that no matter how much her deceit hurt me, I'd die for her if I had to. She's my son's mother, and he needs her more than anyone else on this planet.

Leaning toward her door, the floor creaks, and I instantly flatten myself against the wall, holding my breath. I want to have the drop on whoever's in there, not the other way around.

There's silence for a few moments and then a soft cry. It's the last straw. I jump through the opening, in a fighter stance, ready to stab to death whomever I need to, so I can save Bethany.

The room's empty; her window's even closed and locked securely. It's just her, tossing and turning while grumbling. She's dreaming, but whatever it is, it's making her scared or hurt.

I could walk away right now, go back to sleep on the couch and pretend like this never even happened. I don't need to worry myself over her comfort, and I shouldn't want to after what she pulled. But I do.

Her being upset makes it hard for me to breathe for some reason. It's confusing and infuriating. I'm a criminal, an outlaw; I don't care about shit if it doesn't concern me or my club.

Yet, she concerns me. She digs at my heart that I once believed didn't exist, and that's answer enough. I need to comfort her. I don't have to fuck her or have a relationship with her, but, in this moment, I can at least make sure she's okay. There were so many dreams and so many times I'd wished someone would've done the same for me.

Standing beside her bed, I watch her a few moments more until she calls out loudly, scrunching her face up. In pain or in sadness, I wonder? Who knows, but something is definitely not right in her head tonight.

I can't help but think it's me in there, terrorizing her. She's acted pretty scared and nervous since I've arrived, but, honestly, I've relished it. I've taken each little terrified look she's sent at some of my remarks and have added them inside, collecting bits and pieces, letting them offer me what small comfort they can.

Revenge...I love getting payback when it's due to me, but how do you take out your hurt and anger on the mother of your child? I kill her for the shit she pulled, and, then suddenly, I'm the bad guy in the equation. I refuse to be the villain in my son's eyes. I may not be some real hero out there, but to him, I will do everything in my power to look like I should be one.

I could shake her, rouse her enough to pull her free, but I don't. I'm stupid, I want to feel her against me, and this is offering me the perfect excuse to do just that. Pulling the puffy comforter away from the pillows, I climb into the bed next to her.

One hand on her shoulder, I place my other palm to her face. She whimpers and the sound's beautiful. I'd love to have her whimpering underneath me, but in pain and pleasure combined.

"Bethany." It comes out in a bit of a grumble. I'm still tired and watching her half-naked has me flexing and hard.

She doesn't wake, so I stroke over the side of her face, calling her again. "Little Daydream...wake up, baby."

"Night?" Her eyes crack open, dazed and confused. I'm sure she's wondering what I'm doing in her bed and touching her as well.

"I'm here, you're safe."

Tears well up, her pouty lip trembling, and then she's in my arms. Her own wrapped around my neck, head against my chest as sobs wrack her body.

"Shh, shh, you're okay. I got you, baby, don't worry."

"Oh God," she whispers, still crying.

"Was it really that bad? What happened?"

"I-I don't want to talk about it. If I talk about it, it becomes worse, because then it's real."

"Fine. Just tell me...was it me making you like this?"

"You? No-no-no...it was...it was my father," she admits, her warm breath fanning over my pecs. A few shuddering breaths and her tears begin to dry up.

I lie back, pulling her on me until I can wrap my arms around her securely. We l like that, chest to chest for what feels like hours. Truth is, I have no idea how much time passes; eventually, we both drift off to sleep.

It's in the early morning when she's sleeping soundly that I crawl free from her touch, wrapping the blankets around her cozily. That was close enough for now. I have to keep reminding myself that I hate her for what she did, that we could never be.

I would never be able to trust her to even give her a chance.

However, I can't help but wonder why it was her that got pregnant with my child. I'd lied to her about being careful. I wasn't; in fact, I was careless. No woman ever got pregnant no matter how many times I fucked them...and then there was her.

BETHANY

I wake to a cold bed and groggy thoughts of Nightmare holding me all night long. Part of me believes that last night never happened, but I know it did. My bed still smells like him.

Rolling over in his spot, I deeply breathe in his scent. It's been a very long time since a man was in my bed in any form, and smelling him has my body wound tight, senses in overdrive.

My hand crawls over my stomach, fingers almost going into my panties when I get a wake-up call.

"Momma?"

"Hmmm," I groan, rolling over to my back.

"Cereal's wready"

Shit. That means there's a mess from hell in my kitchen and probably no milk left. I thought we talked about him fixing his own breakfast; it never works out for either one of us.

"'Kay, I'll be right there."

Clumsily, I head for the bathroom, taking care of business and washing my face with cold water, so I'm awake enough to mop up the milk that I know is coating my kitchen floor. At least it wasn't eggs this time; cleaning those up suck.

When I round the corner, I'm met with essentially two Nightmares—one big version and one mini version. They're sitting at the kitchen table, both staring into the living room at cartoons while they eat cereal. Surprisingly, there's no mess either.

"Hey," I mumble, heading for the coffee machine. It's a fresh pot. Neither of them glance in my direction, zoned out on *Transformers*. I pour myself a cup, adding in a splash of cream and two scoopfuls of sugar.

Throwing away the empty sugar container, I come across what looks like an entire roll of wet paper towels in the trash as well. My gaze lands on Nightmare.

"Did Maverick make breakfast?" I ask, curiously, and Nightmare finally glances over at me and nods.

"Yep. I woke up when he yelled, 'Oh shit.' Turns out the milk was a little heavy for him."

And being a typical man, he used every paper towel in sight to clean it up versus just grabbing the mop. But one thing stands out; he got up, helped Mav, and then cleaned up the mess. He actually cleaned it up and let me sleep.

Checking the clock, it reads nine a.m., and it makes me giggle.

"You all right?" His eyebrow tips up, concerned with my weird behavior. He doesn't understand the only time I ever get to sleep in is when Princess visits every few months, and I rarely do it then too. I could jump up and down and cheer right now.

Daydream

"Fine." Grinning, I bring my cup of coffee with me and sit in the chair between them. I have cartoons to watch with my son and my baby daddy. Never in a million years, did I imagine I'd ever be able to say that.

CHAPTER 12

She dreams more often

than she sleeps.

- Jonny OX

"When wiw he be back?"

"We've been over this Mav; he had to go home to where he lives so he could work." He, meaning Nightmare. We've been over this daily since Nightmare left.

"But when wiw he be back?"

"Soon."

"Soon," he grumbles, copying me as his gaze turns out the window to watch the scenery as we drive.

It's weird, but I miss him, too. Sure, there were many nights I thought of him over the years, but this past weekend went well—really well.

He was a dick to me Friday when he first arrived, but then I cooked him dinner. The next night he held me when he didn't have to. It was nice and different. It felt like we were a family, and that's the scary thing, because I loved it, and I know I can't have it. He may have offered me comfort, but he still hates me.

We get back to the apartment, and I give Princess a call. She's another one pissed at me. She has every right to be; it still sucks, though.

"Hey."

"Hey, you still mad at me?"

"I told you, I'm not mad. I'm disappointed; it's different. I wish you would've told me from the beginning. It almost feels like you didn't trust me enough to have your back."

"Of course, I trust you. You have to look at it from my point of view, too, though. I had just found out I was pregnant. I was tripping, freaking out over my life changing, and Nightmare's words hurt me. Of course, I took him at face value; I didn't know him well enough not to."

"And you do now?"

"Hell no. I wish I could change how I went about things, but if I'm honest with myself, I would probably do the exact same thing again. I didn't have options when Maverick's existence surfaced. I had to bite the bullet, grow the fuck up and take care of the both of us, so that's exactly what I did."

152

She sighs. "I know. It's just...now Viking thinks I kept this from him and is questioning me on what else I've kept from him. You need to start coming down here and being around the club."

"Why would I do that? Those guys despise me for keeping Maverick away from Nightmare. I'm the bad guy, remember?"

"They only see it from his side of view; they don't know you or your story like I do. Start coming around so they can see for themselves you're not trying to keep him away any longer. Trust me, you'll want them on your side. It may suck for a little while, because, I'll be real with you, they most likely will be jerks. Not to Mav, but to you. Once you choke through it, they'll have your back. Most of all, they'll have Maverick's, and I know how important family is to you, B."

"I don't care if they support me in any way, but you're right about one thing. I do want my son around family, and I know the club is loyal to their own. I don't necessarily want Maverick growing up to be a biker, but I do want him surrounded by people who'll have his best interest at heart."

"That's us."

"I know, Prissy; I know. Nightmare was coming back up here this weekend, but maybe I'll see if I can take it off and go there instead. He saved me a lot of money being here last weekend to hang out with Mav while I worked."

"See, Nightmare being in your life could be good in multiple ways."

"I know, I keep reminding myself of the benefits. It's still hard to be around him, and even more so, now that he hates me."

"He doesn't hate you, Bethany."

"Oh no, believe me, he does. He sat right across from me at a table and told me he'd like to peel my skin from my flesh. Pretty sure that equals hate."

She chuckles, and I huff.

"He has it so bad for you."

"Yeah, like the man may kill me in my sleep one night."

"No as in he was all over you to get in your pants again, and now he's threatening you with bodily harm. He knows you're the mother of his child. He fucking wants you."

"Yeah, well, I'm not going to make any bets or hold my breath on it."

"Oh yeah, what was that bet you made me when this whole thing started? Oh no, it wasn't a bet...but I remember your words." She laughs, then in a snooty tone, pretends to mock me. "'Fine, but I'm not fucking any of them'." She bursts out laughing like a hyena. "So busted. We have DNA proof you're full of shit."

"You're such a bitch, Prissy."

She laughs again, at my expense, and I laugh, too. I'm just happy the guilt trip for not telling her about Night is letting up.

"I am, but you still love me."

"Ugh, God knows why, but I do."

"Good. I love you, too. Now let me know if you can come this weekend. I'm sure Nightmare will have you staying at his house; but if not, you can stay at mine."

"There's no way I'm staying with him. I want to keep my skin, thank you."

"You'll have to fight with *him* about that, but anyway, let me know."

"I will."

"Okay, byeeeeee."

"Bye." I hang up, rolling my eyes. I am happy that we ended the call on a good note, though. It's hard when your best friend is upset with you.

It's also time I start planning Maverick's birthday party. Usually Princess would come to visit, and I'd make a cake for him, but I have a feeling Nightmare will want to be involved this time around.

Each day that passes, I continue with the daily texts. I always send a new picture of Maverick and let Nightmare know of anything significant. Usually, it's just a small message from Mav. Today's was: Maverick wants to know if you like meatballs and with sauce or no sauce?

Random, I know, but I'm hoping it makes Nightmare feel a little closer to his son. Maverick thinks it's neat, too, and has started helping me pick out which picture to send. Nightmare could think it's stupid for all I know, but, as a parent, pictures mean something.

At least they do to me. It's like little perfect moments frozen in time that you can look back on and remember. I could be having a rough day and look at Mav surrounded in bubbles, and no matter how blue I am, it makes me smile. I'm crossing my fingers that they do the same when I send Nightmare his daily text from us.

My phone beeps.

Nightmare: Yes and yes. Tell him I'll see him tomorrow and I'm teaching him to play my drum set. Be safe driving.

Me: I will.

He argued with me about us staying with Princess. I knew he would, but I still had to try. It's awkward enough, but at least staying with Princess would provide some sort of barrier.

I'm going to pick up groceries before we leave so I can cook dinner tomorrow night. I think it'll be a good way to break the ice. I think when it boils down to it, it's the small things that really matter. Dinner may seem like nothing to some, but Nightmare and Maverick haven't gotten the chance to sit down at dinner together. Last weekend was the first time, and while I can't make up for everything Night has missed, this is one small thing I can give them both.

All of this is new, and I'm lost. I'm not used to worrying about sharing my son with anyone. The thought was always in the back of my mind that one day it could happen. That's not true; the actual thought was that there was a chance of Nightmare showing up and taking my son from me completely if he were to find out the truth.

So, this visiting or whatever it is we're doing, I'll gladly do my part, because, in my heart, I know it could be so much worse. He could want nothing to do with our son ever, or he could take him away from me completely. Nightmare has the means to just disappear if he wanted too. He's an outlaw, and those types of men do what they want and know how to do it without getting caught.

With a sigh, I down the large glass of wine and pray that I'm able to sleep tonight. I'll definitely need my wits about me tomorrow. Who knows what kind of mood my baby daddy will be in. Not only that, but I have to face his brothers, and some of them are as ruthless as he's known to be. Fingers crossed I make it home in one piece.

NIGHTMARE

Having them in my space is strange; not bad, just different. Not like I'm here much anyhow. I'm usually at the club or gone doing something—a run, a gig, whatever.

Maverick's discovered my drums and thinks they're pretty bitchin'. Those are my words, not his. His were more along the lines of "Ummm...wow." Bitchin' sounds better in my mind. His mom would have my ass if I taught him that word, though, so we'll save it for when he's older.

I'm not going to lie to myself either. Having Bethany floating around in the kitchen, cooking dinner, is pretty fucking nice. I haven't brought anyone here except for a few brothers. Club whores are meant to be kept at the club, not brought home.

I don't touch any of them anyhow. I haven't been abstinent by any means, but I hit it out of town. Bethany or my son will never have to worry about running into past pussy.

I like it that way; less bullshit for everyone involved. The gigs and runs help make that possible. I don't know what the hell to do now, though.

Nearly two weeks ago I had getting in Bethany's pants, and possibly keeping her, on my mind. Last week after the news of my son being kept from me came out in the open, I hated all women. This weekend, I just have no idea where I sit with anything.

Part of me still hates Bethany. I think I'll always have resentment toward her for that. However, other thoughts have been creeping in as well. Like how I'm unbelievably grateful to have a kid and a son at that. Also, that she's the mother of my child, and so far, appears to be a damn good mother to my kid.

What more can a man ask for, but a woman that takes care of your kid well. I could go into little details like decent whiskey, tight pussy, etc. but that's all irrelevant when you get down to the shit that really matters in life.

Do I still want to fuck Bethany? Of course, I do; I'm a red-blooded male in his prime. I've thought of fucking her to make her mine. Then I thought about hate fucking her, then fucking her and killing her, then more hate fucking. Now I'm almost to the point of make-up fucking.

I'm pretty sure if she would suck my cock dry for the next few years, I could find it in my heart to forgive her. It's shallow, but I'm not a fake motherfucker. Every man out there with a dick who loves women would feel the same way. They're just pussies and won't admit it; I'm not.

So, here I sit, at the club having a drink and thinking while B and my kid are at my house—hopefully, sound asleep. She thought she could fight me on where they're staying. Not a chance. She owes me, and she knows it.

It's gonna be my way on a lot of shit for the foreseeable future, so she needs to come to terms with it. I should be at home with them, but I need time to clear my head after spending a quiet evening with them both.

"Another?" Blaze gestures to my empty bottle.

Shrugging, I nod. "Sure, fuck it."

"How you holdin' up, lad?" Scot stares at me curiously. He's the oldest member here at the clubhouse, and I've ridden with him for many years. He was sort of in charge when we were Nomads; but here, he's my brother—another officer in the club.

"I haven't strangled her yet."

"Aye." He chuckles. "Have ye fucked 'er again?"

That's the question of the night it seems. Every brother I've come across has asked the same damn thing. Fuckers, all thinking with their cocks.

"Nope, sure haven't."

"Stronger man than I." He laughs again, finishing his draft. "Time I go check on my ol' lady."

"Be safe, brother."

"Aye, you too, lad." He shakes my hand and heads out.

His ol' lady runs the local bar about twenty minutes down the road, and Scot always shows up when it's near closing time. After Viking's father shot her, Scot's been stuck up her ass and with good reason. I'd be even worse if it were my ol' lady, I suppose.

Blaze sets the fresh, cold beer in front of me, and I gulp down a large swig.

"So she came back, huh?"

I grunt, not saying anything really. Everyone knows my business and that shit drives me crazy. I don't do drama, especially when it comes to the club.

"Look, I know I haven't been around you as long as Scot or say Viking, but I'm your brother nonetheless. I just want you to be happy, and I'm glad she's giving you the chance to be in your kid's life."

I've never had an issue with Blaze. He's Viking's cousin and very loyal. But his admission makes my respect for him rise. Stupid, how just a few words can make you respect a man, but it's true.

"Appreciate that."

Daydream

He nods. "But what are you doin' here, brother? Your son and a woman, who you no doubt care for, is right down the street at your house."

"I know; fuck, I know. We had a good night, I just needed to breathe."

"Ah, yeah, that's a big change. We're here for you man, any one of us has your back if you need something."

"Even a shovel to bury a body?"

"As long as it's not the kids, then fuckin' right."

"If it's the kids, I'd be slicing and dicing whoever is responsible."

"And I'd help you in a heartbeat."

Ex better watch out. Blaze seems to want to fill his spot as my closest friend. Not that it would happen, but Blaze has opened my eyes to him a little more tonight.

Sapphire Knight

CHAPTER 13

It will cost you nothing to dream,

and everything not to.

-GeniusQuotes.net

Church, four days later...

"We have a run coming up this weekend. Nightmare and Chaos, are you both still good for it?"

We both nod. It sucks because I'll have to miss my visit with my son, but I'm not going to shoot down business. It's my responsibility as an officer in the club. I'll have to make a trip up during the week or something to see Maverick it looks like.

"Prez." Blaze interrupts.

"Yeah?" Everyone's gaze shoots to Blaze.

"How about I head out with Chaos this weekend?"

"There a problem?" Viking grumbles.

"Nah, but Nightmare's just gettin' to know his son. He needs off weekends more right now than the rest of us."

My mouth drops open at his admission. I'm stunned, but I guess I shouldn't be; we're a family and try to step up when someone else needs it. I didn't realize it was me that needed it though. I try not to ask anything of my brothers besides their loyalty.

"You good with that, Night?" Prez asks, and I nod, confirming. Hell yeah, I am.

I'm so damn grateful. I didn't even have to say a word, and a brother stepped up for me. It's another reason why the club means so much, and I've dedicated a large portion of my life to it.

"I appreciate it."

No one says anything, blowing it off. It's what we all do when someone says thank you like it doesn't even need to be mentioned. It's true, though. I am thankful, and now I get to visit my family—my other family, that is.

I guess that's what Bethany and Maverick are, after all—my family. It's been a long time since I've had someone actually blood-related to me. Ever since my father was killed, family has become whoever I chose, whoever has earned the title in my eyes.

"It's settled, then." My thoughts are interrupted. "Chaos and Blaze will do this weekend's run. We have a club run coming up in two months. We all need to be on board, as it's to welcome in a new Prez to an Oath Keepers charter."

"Taking over the motherfuckin' world." Bronx snickers and we either chuckle or roll our eyes.

He's young but has come a long way since we first came across him. Bronx was a part of the giant shit show when everything went down with Scot's ol' lady and Princess got held up at the bar. Viking overtook the old club. The Widow Makers MC and Bronx was one that patched over, along with Blaze, Torch, Smokey, and Odin.

"Night, you planning to get B to move down here with you?"

"Yep, working on it," I answer Viking, everyone's attention on me, yet again. I hate that shit.

"Bet. Let us know so we can make sure we're available to help move her shit if you need it."

"I will."

"Now, back to the pussy. Anymore issues?"

Torch speaks up, "Everything was smooth this last week, and the girls turned good profit as did we."

"Thank Christ; last thing I want to deal with is pussy problems."

"Aye, yer ol' lady holdin' out on ye then?" Scot riles and Viking growls causing the rest of us to snicker to ourselves.

We're quiet because Viking has a temper like no other. While he wouldn't put a bullet in our skulls, the fucker would damn sure throw a punch, and he's no small man to tangle with. The first time I met him, he was fighting off five or six guys at once. He wasn't winning, but that was beside the point.

"Don't be worryin' about my shit, and I won't worry about your wrinkly ass," he replies, and Scot laughs loudly. "All right then, everyone good?"

We all reply with yes and aye. Viking slams the gavel down and we head out. Another successful church meeting for the books, and now it's time to have a drink with the brothers. It's one of the best parts about having church; we take a moment afterward to visit.

I plant my ass on the barstool as my phone chimes with a text from Bethany. Opening the message, it's a new picture. This one is different than her usual daily text. The photo isn't of just Maverick; it's of them both and fuck if it isn't my favorite yet.

B: 2nd Birthday, he took a bite of cake and then smeared it all over my face. Speaking of, Maverick has a Birthday coming up!

I stare at the photo, grinning like a goddamn fool and decide to make it the screen saver on my phone. They're both covered in blue frosting, and it's hilarious. Maverick looks so proud of himself while Bethany's mouth is gaping open in shock. Whoever snapped the picture, timed it perfectly. *Probably Princess.*

For the first time in two and a half weeks, I look at her and don't become angry when doing so. Has to mean something, right? She's a natural beauty, stealing my breath away in a ponytail with frosting smeared across her cheeks.

"Hey, Scot, can I borrow your truck and trailer this weekend?"

"Aye, ye need some help?"

"Nah, I'm good. I'm going to load it up with Bethany's furniture while she's at work. Figure she can't argue with me if she's not there."

He chuckles and removes a key off his keyring. "Take it anytime, lad. Can't wait to see thee lass spit fire over this one."

"Not sure it'll be fire, but no doubt she'll be pissed I'm moving her shit without telling her. I'm counting on her anger, looking forward to it actually."

"You're going to turn her into one of those psycho bitches that chop your dick off in the middle of the night," Bronx interrupts.

"I'm counting on that, too. Only I'll keep my cock and enjoy driving her crazy at the same time." I smirk and motion to Blaze for a whiskey.

"Want me to come with you?" he asks, and I shake my head.

"No, I can handle her, and she doesn't have a lot of stuff. Mav is easy; I'm going to tell him he can have a puppy."

The guys around me all laugh, knowing I'm playing dirty by swaying my son with a dog. I'm not above getting down and dirty, though; I'll do what I need to. I didn't become an outlaw by participating in a fucking hotdog eating contest. I became this way because I'm a bastard. I'm not above doing what I have to, for what I want. Hell, I'll get my son a damn piglet if it's needed; I'm not opposed to bribery.

"Nightmare," Viking grumbles, coming to stand behind me.

"Brother?"

"I just got a call. Prospect says one of the girls was roughed up pretty bad last night. He just found her and had to take her to see the doc. I want you and Saint to go pay a visit to the dumb fuck that was stupid enough to take it too far."

"I'll go with Night," Blaze suggests, eavesdropping on me and his cousin.

"No, you stay here. This will take a certain kind of finesse. I want an example made," Viking grits, evil dancing in his eyes, and I know he wants us to make the guy hurt really bad.

"No problem, but Saint and I...you know, we each do shit differently." I clench my hand, feeling the thick scar on my palm. The mark from holding the door closed as a teen has never gone away. It's a constant reminder of how I became the man I am today, of what my methods are. I like to watch them burn, to smell the stench and hear their cries of agony.

"I know, brother. Let Saint play for a while, then do it your way to get rid of the evidence."

In other words, let Saint get bloody, and then I can light the fucker on fire. The hard part will be controlling Saint though. He goes a little psycho when he sees blood; the brother practically bathes in it when given the chance. I tend to stay cleaner. I save getting dirty for when I'm working on bikes or sweaty when I'm hitting the drums for a set.

"And Sinner?" He's usually attached to Saint's side to keep him in check. They balance each other out or some shit. The point is, you don't see Saint out and about much without him. I'm not about to have to leash his ass. I'm not Saint's keeper.

"Sinner's preoccupied. Like I said, let Saint have some fun, and he'll be fine. It's when you hold him back, he loses it. You know how he is."

I nod. Looks like it's time to get bloody and teach someone a lesson.

It didn't take much to find the fucker who messed up one of the whores. It never does, though. We have a nose for sniffing out filthy fuckers. This guy was a repeat, so the prospect recognized him immediately.

Punching the weasel is cathartic. I love taking care of issues with my fists or with fire. He flies to the floor, and Saint's eyes go a little crazy, and he cackles, "Can I?" He stares at the man who's gasping for breath at my feet.

I hit pretty damn hard, and he's only experienced a small taste of my anger. I could tear his body apart with my hands, break bone after bone if I wanted. Instead of crushing his skull with my boot, I decide to heed Viking's suggestion about holding my brother back.

"Go for it."

At my go ahead, Saint kneels beside the guy and removes his blade and begins to stab the piece of shit woman beater to death. He plunges the sharp knife into the man a good fifteen times through protests, cries, and gurgles until finally, Saint drops the weapon to his side. His hands go to the weasel's throat, squeezing until the guy stops making noises.

Next, they trail to his chest, smearing the blood everywhere before collecting what he can in his hands and wiping it over his own arms. It reminds me of some crazed Indian ritual or something. The brother has some serious loose screws.

Saint's fucking crazy. Did I mention that before? It's completely opposite to his preppy, pretty boy model appearance too. One look at him, and you'd think he was a rock star or something, not a serial killer on a leash.

He laughs again. "Want me to peel his skin off next?"

This is why he and Viking get along so well. Viking is off his rocker when it comes to people pissing him off too.

"No man, he's already gone. It's a shame, too. Really would've liked to burn him alive; it wouldn't have ended so quickly."

His smile drops, and his gaze grew serious as he stared at the lifeless body before him. "Viking said he wanted him to bleed."

"You killed it, literally," I snort and grab a can of old gasoline I'd found in the garage when we first arrived.

Saint grins, grabbing his favorite hunting knife and backs away as I begin to soak the mutilated body in the petrol. We leave a trail from the body to the front door, where I use my trusty zippo to start the fire that will erase any implication we were ever in the house.

The body will be too far gone by the time anyone gets here that the authorities will never be able to tell it was us.

"You good?" I ask, a little concerned with his appearance.

We climb on our bikes, and I wait for Saint to get situated. He looks somewhere between a horror movie and a car-crash victim. The blood's already beginning to dry on his arms, turning a reddish-brown, and he reeks of the metallic scent that blood gives off.

A shower may not help. He needs a deep cleaning to scrub that shit off. I feel like I should take him to the carwash and hose him down, but Viking and Sinner wouldn't find that as amusing as I would.

I'm sure Sinner will be all over my ass when we get back, for letting Saint's "crazy" out to play. The man's like a demented angel of some sort—pretty-boy looks with blond hair and light gray eyes. I'm sure if you peeled that layer away you'd find a soul as black as can be. How Sinner cares for him so much, I'll never understand.

"Yep, I am. You ready to take off?"

I nod, and the rumble from our bikes drown out the nearby chirping birds as we take off for the clubhouse. Business is done—for now.

"Hey." My eyes rake over B from top to bottom. She's dressed for work but still looks sexy as fuck.

"Hi. Perfect timing." She steps back so I can come into her apartment.

"I liked the pictures this week." Muttering, I follow her into the kitchen.

She smiles, her eyes lighting up. "Oh yeah? He's pretty great, huh?"

"Yeah," I agree as my son comes tearing down the hallway at my voice. He flies into my arms, and my body feels warm all over because of his tiny embrace. You never know what you've been missing until you finally have it.

"I missed yow." He squeezes me tighter, and I chuckle.

Around him, I don't have to be so serious. He doesn't know the dark side of me, and I love that fact. I want him to know me as dad, not Nightmare.

"Missed you, too, kid." I squeeze him back, and he acts like I squish him, sticking his tongue out and rolling his eyes back.

Bethany's smile grows. "Thanks for being here. I should be off around six thirty when the last girl clocks on for the dinner shift."

"No rush. We're going to hang out and maybe eat some ice cream. I brought the Monster Truck movie Maverick asked for. Besides, you should just quit."

She laughs, rolling her eyes. "Yeah, right. Maybe someday in a far-off land when fairies pay my bills, then I'll quit and eat ice cream with y'all." She winks, and I smirk. Little does she know, but her ass will be quitting whether she likes it or not. She'll find out when she gets home, and all her shit's packed and loaded on the trailer outside.

"I'll be back later; you two have fun, and Night, call if you need anything."

"I will."

"Ummm...we wiw. Love you, Momma"

"Love you, buddy." She blows him a kiss and grabs her purse.

She's off to work, and it's just me and little man left at the kitchen table. I may as well not waste any time. Turning to him, I grin. "So...you like puppies, Maverick?"

Sapphire Knight

CHAPTER 14

You can't rush something you

want to last forever.

- Love Quotes

BETHANY

I pull up to the apartment, noticing a truck parked across a few spots with a trailer attached. The bed and the trailer are packed full of what looks to be my couch amongst other belongings. Weird cause I could've sworn our building was full, and it's even stranger that it looks like my furniture secured under the bungee cords and rope.

If Nightmare replaced my furniture, I'm going to be pissed. That takes a lot of nerve coming to someone's house and getting rid of their things.

Getting out of my car, I approach the vehicle on my way to my front door, paying closer attention. Yep, there's my ugly yellow lamp that's normally on the table beside my bed. But what in the hell is it doing out here, packed up? Did something happen? Oh, God, was there a water leak or something?

Fuck! My heart begins to beat quicker as I jog to the front door. It's locked, so I find the right key and burst in, drawing Maverick and Nightmare's gaze and a...puppy?

"Hey, what's going on?" I ask in a rush, closing the door. The dog runs at me, tail wagging like crazy. "Whose dog?" Bending down, I scratch behind his little floppy ears, because, duh, it's a puppy, and they're adorable.

"It's Maverick's," Night replies and Maverick nods his head crazily, a huge smile overtaking his face.

"But we can't have dogs here."

"Not my problem." The broody bastard shrugs, and I bite my tongue from calling him a dick.

I'm going to be the horrible mommy by taking the damn puppy away from my child. Not like I wouldn't give my son a dog or cat, but they'll kick us out of here, and a place to live is far more important. Not to mention dog food and vet bills—a luxury I can't fathom right now.

"We need to talk," I huff and glance around, noticing my furniture is indeed not here. "Did something happen? Why is everything outside?"

"We packed, Momma!" Mav yells and jumps up, coming to bother the puppy.

"I see that, but why. What happened?" I grin. It's completely fake and forced. I know none of this was my son's idea, and I won't take it out on *him*. Nightmare is in an entirely different boat though.

"You're moving." Nightmare shrugs, like I should already know this.

"Ummm...no, we're not." My eyebrows rise.

"Pretty sure I told you before; you're coming to my place."

"And we get a puppy!" Maverick cheers, making me cringe.

"Shit, shit, shit. This isn't happening. I told you no. I distinctly remember saying the actual word 'no'."

"And like I said, *not my problem.*"

"It is if you don't unload that truck and put everything back where I had it all."

"Nah, it's only an issue if you don't come to terms. Me, Maverick and that dog," he points to my feet at the little puppy wiggling around, "along with the truck full of shit are leaving tomorrow morning. The real question here is, are you coming with us?"

I'm so angry at him right now for putting me in this position, I can't speak. I storm for the bathroom as tears fill my eyes. I just want to scream and punch him, but I won't let my child witness me behaving like that. This man is infuriating! What gives him the right to walk in and suddenly think he can change my life however he sees fit?

He's insane, packing up my apartment while I'm at work. And he bought Maverick a puppy...a fucking puppy! Who does that shit?

Nightmare does, obviously.

This is how my life is going to be, too, for the remainder of time until Maverick turns eighteen and moves out. Fifteen more years of this overbearing alpha taking control of everything. I'm going to go batshit crazy at this rate.

Pulling my phone out, I turn it on and hit the speed dial number for Princess. She's probably the only person who will understand what's happening right now, and she'll let me vent without freaking out over whatever I say.

"What?" It's Viking. *Shit.* Not who I was expecting.

Clearing my throat, I huff out, "Is Princess there?"

"Yeah, but she's busy."

Dickhead. I'm surrounded by them as of late, it seems. Is it something in the water all of a sudden? Christ!

"Well, will she be un-busy soon-ish?"

"Is it important?" He's just like speaking to Night, I swear.

"Well, I'm trying not to stab your brother in front of my child at the moment, so I'd say yeah."

He chuckles. The badass over-the-top Viking, just laughs at my frustration.

"Lemme' give you some advice, B. Whatever my brother's doing, just suck it up and go with it."

"Even if that includes giving up my apartment, my job, and basically what little bit of a life I have?" It leaves me in a dramatic huff, pissed to my core.

"Yep," he responds, and I hang up the phone. He's just as nutty as ol' boy in my living room. Fucking control freaks.

The bathroom door opens, and the small space grows tiny with Nightmare's overly large presence. He comes in and closes the door behind him, making the fit even tighter.

"You calm the fuck down yet?"

He stares at me like I'm the one being irrational. Thankfully the tears went away speaking to Viking, but the anger not so much. It's still there. "Calm down? You seriously have some freaking nerve."

His hand flies up, pointing at my chest. "Oh, I have nerve? How about you look in the mirror, dollface. Pot calling the kettle black, dontcha think?"

"You're going to hold this over my head for the rest of my life, aren't you?" I ask outright. Fuck beating around the bush at this point.

He steps closer, my back hitting the counter as his thigh comes between my own. The position is unbelievably intimate, and if I drop from my tippy-toes to standing normally, I'd be pressed against his leg. I can't handle him touching my clit right now in any form; it's hard enough with him in the same room.

I draw in a deep breath at his scent surrounding me. It's the type of manliness that envelops you and makes you forget about anything else. Did I mention before that he has a beard, too? That detail alone makes my insides twirl.

Leaning closer, he brushes his nose up the side of my cheek causing my stomach to tighten up in anticipation. Eventually, his dark gaze comes to mine; the silver line standing out in stark contrast as our noses nearly touch. He grumbles low enough it comes out as a threat, even with grape soda on his breath. He's serious. "If I have to. I'll use it for however long I need to."

Tears form again as I swallow and my throat grows dry. He fights dirty, and he doesn't care who it affects. I should've known him finding out about our son would be a losing battle. In a sense, I did, but I hoped it wouldn't come to this—him taking control over me and my life.

Swallowing, I whisper as a tear falls. "If you make us leave with you, I'll never be happy there."

He backs up, an evil grin coming over his stern features. "Baby, that's where you think I care about your feelings. I don't." He shakes his head as another tear tumbles over my cheek. "You'll grab your purse, suck it the fuck up, and move your shit. You know why, Bethany? I'll tell you why. You fuckin' owe me. That's why."

His fingers go to my chin, and he tips my head up so I meet his gaze and he drives it home. "You kept my kid from me for three fucking years, and I'm playing nice. Oh, baby, I'm being *so* fucking nice to you, you have no clue the hell I could rain down over you."

His hand drops, and he blinks, glancing away. "Fix your face; it won't work on me. Be ready at six a.m. Set your phone alarm if you have too. I don't give a fuck, but Maverick, that dog, and I will be loaded up no later than six fifteen."

Swallowing again, I nod shortly, my eyes falling to the floor. I can't look at him right now because, in this moment, I hate him all over again.

He hasn't changed; he's still as heartless as he was when I first met him. The beast I thought I'd tame, the broken man, meant for me. I was so fucking wrong.

He leaves the bathroom, and I pull my phone out to set my alarm. I damn sure won't be letting him go anywhere with my son without me. While I'm at it, I send a text to the day manager, Brenda.

Me: I'm sorry to do this to you on short notice, but I won't be back to work again. Thank you for everything you've done for me, giving me a job, working with my schedule and sick days.

Brenda: Oh no, Bethany! I'm sorry to see you go, I hope you're all right.

Me: I am, my life is just changing and I can't stop it.

Brenda: Life happens honey, I understand. You and little guy will be in my prayers.

Me: Thank you.

Thank God someone's praying for me; Lord knows I'm going to need it where I'm going.

I wake up at five a.m. and get the groceries packed and clean the apartment as much as I can. It's not great, but I'm hopeful the landlord won't charge too much. He's been nice, letting me make payments for the deposit and what not in the past, so hopefully, he'll do the same with whatever bill I have left.

I can't believe Nightmare's making me break my lease. This will only add more to my already full load of trying to support Maverick and me. I need to see about getting another job this week. Something where I won't have to leave Maverick too much but will give me some money to pay the bills I'll have haunting me with this impromptu move.

Maverick and the puppy ride with Nightmare in whoever's truck he's borrowing, and I follow behind in my car, alone. It's terrible, but secretly, I'm hoping Mav goes on one of his 'no' sprees for like an hour straight. I need to get some sort of payback, and while that's nothing major, it's enough to bring me a bit of satisfaction. Nightmare is nuts if he thinks it's going to be all rainbows and sunshine having us in his space.

He's never dealt with a sick kid who pukes and cries for three days straight or a toddler who decides to make breakfast once a week and destroys the kitchen in the process. He'll learn, and while he's figuring it all out, I'll be saving any money I can. That way when he gets sick of playing daddy, I'm one step ahead and ready. I hope for Maverick's sake that he never realizes just how much of an asshole his father really is.

CHAPTER 15

Love is not an emotion,

it is your very existence.

-Rumi

"So, how's it going?" Prissy sets her soda down, staring at me intently.

I sip from my cherry vodka Sprite and roll my eyes. "It's been a week and the best way I'd describe it is, awkward."

"Still? I figured with some time it would get better or easier."

"He's a good dad, so I'm thankful for that. He's fine with me for the most part, too, but he's still pissed. I know it."

"You did keep his kid from him."

"Fuck, I know, okay. Jesus, I get it. I fucked up majorly, and now I'm paying for it by letting a biker control my life."

"It could be a lot worse; at least Night wants you guys in his life."

"Whose side are you on? You're my best friend, but it's sounding more and more like you're taking his side."

"I'm Switzerland, okay. I think you both screwed up, and you're both having to learn how to fix it now. Look, I don't agree with how he got you here. But, I am grateful that you are. I missed you. I feel like he's brought my best friend back to me, and he does sorta earn points from me for doing it."

"So, you are on his side."

She huffs, pushing the soda away and drinks from her beer. "I'm always on your side first."

"Mmmhmm." I lean against the bar, watching the brothers around the room, chatting, laughing, and drinking. London asked if Maverick could have a happy meal and a playdate with her daughter. Of course, I agreed, so here I am, having my own playdate.

Some twat walks by Nightmare, running her hand over his chest, saying something in his ear. He shakes his head and moves her hand off.

I smirk, my gaze shooting to Prissy. "Who's the hood rat?" I nod and she groans.

"Ugh, it's Honey. She's a club slut. She's been after Nightmare and Viking since she first showed up. I already put her in her place with Vike. Looks like you need to do the same."

"Why should I care? If he wants that, maybe he'll forget about me."

"Well, because that's Nightmare, Bethany. Wake up, sweet cheeks. You may be pissed at him, but that's your baby daddy. You don't want some club whore sniffing around him, even if he does brush her off."

"Seriously, he's a big boy; he can tell her no. He's never needed me to stand up for him, and he doesn't now."

"B, I'm telling you, don't let it fester. It'll drive you crazy to see her hit on him every single time you're here at the same time he is. You guys have a fresh start; she's just a dirty vagina trying to screw that chance up."

I snort at her description and a few brothers glance at us. Blaze winks, and I grin. Finishing off my drink, I ponder over what Princess says. I know she'd never lead me astray; she always has my best interests at heart, so I take her words seriously.

"Ready then?" I smile mischievously, and her concern turns to a smirk full of trouble. She knows me too well.

"Always."

Heading straight for Nightmare, I garner the brother's attention as I pass by. Everyone's curious to see what I'm going to tell Nightmare. I think they're all wanting to witness some drama, and I'm about to give it to them.

Nightmare remains seated as I approach, tilting his head up to me. Bending before he can react, I place my hands on each of his cheeks and press my lips to his. He's a moody fucker, so I know the women around here don't have the balls to take control when it comes to him.

His palm warms my thigh as it pulls me closer, and the kiss turns from me showing off to something full of lust. Breaking free after a moment, I pant against his lips, wet from my own mouth sucking on them. "Wow," I whisper and blink, remembering my initial purpose. Backing away, I nearly misstep from the kiss that put me in a daze, quickly righting myself.

Honey glares, and I can't help but smirk. At Honey's huff, I pull my arm back and punch her right in her eye. She stumbles backward, clutching her face as a scream of pain breaks free.

"Mine." I declare sternly, turning on my heel and making my way back to my spot next to a giggling Princess. Viking appears impressed, and Nightmare, completely shocked. The other guy's chuckle, amused at my antics, and Odin helps the whore to the bathroom.

"Better?" I mutter and finish off my mixed drink.

"Hell yeah, glad to see you're still the crazy woman I love."

"Shit, baby girl, you just opened up a whole new can of complicated." Blaze shakes his head, in his usual place behind the bar.

"Damn, I thought that's how bikers communicated? Don't you beat on your chests and punch people?"

He snickers. "You're trouble, you know that?"

"I may have been called that a few times in the past."

Princess leans over "Uh, no, she's crazy, Blaze; don't get it twisted. She always has been, and that right there proves she's still the same wild woman I grew up with."

"Hey, I've toned it down a lot, thank you very much."

"Maybe around your kid, but not when it's you and me. No way sister, I see you trying to break free. The good news, B, is that these guys here are even crazier. You fit in here like a lost puzzle piece, just you wait and see."

"If you say so," I sigh.

I haven't really fit in anywhere, ever. I became the crazy party girl prior to getting pregnant, so I could drown out my lack of everything and not care about anything else. That's why Princess and I became so close; she was different like me, her family belonging to a biker club and all.

"Another one?" Blaze grabs my empty glass, and I nod.

Why not? Maverick does have two parents now. I think I've earned that extra drink.

NIGHTMARE

"Fuck was that?" Viking grumbles after Bethany walks off. He's attempting to act serious when I know he's most likely busting up inside over this.

Personally, I'm still shaken from her pulling that shit. "No idea, brother."

"Chick's a goddamn fruit loop." He downs his whiskey. "Can't believe she just claimed your ass in the middle of the clubhouse, too."

Saint laughs beside me, and I growl, thinking about punching him next. No way was she layin' claim. "That was a fuckin' tantrum, that's it. Bitch was showing off for Princess. Anybody claims anyone; it'll be me fucking her until she can't run that damn mouth of hers."

"Trouble in paradise?" he asks, and I glare. He's the only fucker in this place, besides Ex, who has enough guts to give me shit, especially about Bethany.

"She's driving me crazy," I finally admit.

"Crazy is how I'd describe her." He nods, and I grunt.

"She stares at me all innocent and shit at the house. Just wanna bend her over and spank her ass."

"Maybe you should. It'd bypass this bullshit y'all are going through right now. I had to just say fuck it with Princess and make her mine so she'd quit fuckin' around."

And none of us will ever forget it, either. One of the hottest things I've ever seen; not to mention, I had B on my cock right after that went down. Shrugging, I tip my longneck back and finish off the beer.

I'm not sure what I'm going to do about her yet. I'm still pissed inside and want her ass walking on eggshells a while longer, but I'm not sure how much more I can take. This last week she's slept right down the hall from me, and I've held her twice. Her and those fucking dreams, they screw her up in the middle of the night, bad.

Crazy thing is, once I hold her, she sleeps like the dead. I can move around, shower, get dressed, whatever, and nothing wakes her. When she's by herself, she tosses and turns, cries out, you name it. I know because I like to watch her sleep. I witness it every night.

I can't believe she just came over here and pulled that on Honey and me. I have to give Bethany some credit; she completely surprised everyone with that one.

"Your band have a gig this weekend?" Chaos pipes up. He's pretty quiet; one of the reasons why I don't mind him.

"Yeah, out at Shorty's."

"Bet, I'll head over with you. Friday or Saturday?"

"Both."

He nods. "You should get some pussy, take your mind off her." He gestures in Bethany's direction. While that would've sounded good before, it does nothing for me now. The only pussy I want riding my dick belongs to that hotheaded chick that just laid one hell of a kiss on my mouth.

"She smells another bitch on you, you may not wake up in the morning." Viking chuckles, and I grin. It's probably true though. Good thing I won't have to worry about that.

189

"Fucked up." I shake my head.

"How 'bout I tell Odin to babysit. Me and Princess could ride up, you could show B?"

"Not sure she'd like that sort of thing."

Chaos sighs. "Bullshit. Chicks are all over your cock once they see you play."

He has a point; it could win her over a little. I can keep fucking with her here and there and then really hook her. This time when she falls for me, I plan to make sure she never goes anywhere.

"Why you single, Chaos?"

He shrugs. "I had a woman when I first started playing football. She gave me my daughter then split. That was enough for me."

That's right. His daughter visits on her college breaks sometimes. "You haven't been on a run to Alabama in a whole minute. Your kid okay?" That's also how he met our moonshine contact. The stuff here at the club is the real deal—homemade and everything.

"She moved up north with her boyfriend."

"No shit?"

He nods. "He went to play for the Patriots."

"Holy fuck, brother; that's awesome."

"As long as she finishes her degree, I won't kill him," he admits, and we all chuckle. Makes me glad I have a son. Not sure I could handle having a daughter.

Daydream

I get home after Bethany does, and there's dinner already made and waiting for me. I'd never admit it to my brothers, but I love every bit of having her here. I don't know why I want to torment her so badly. My guess is, I'm still hurt. I hate that bullshit. Makes me feel weak, like a chick worried about feelings and shit.

It's true, though. Finding out I had a kid and knew nothing about it, fucked me up inside. I was already screwed up, but this is different. It makes me think that she believes I'm not good enough to be Maverick's father.

However, I will be a good dad to him; I'll make sure of it. I may not be a good person or even a decent man, but I won't let myself fail at being his father. I had enough of that growing up; I won't torment my own kid with that kind of life.

Trekking down the hall, I peek in and check on Mav. He's knocked out, with his feet up on his pillows. Kid sleeps like a wild animal in every direction besides the normal one. It's all good; his mom and I both march to the beat of our own drum, too. Fuck the standards.

Next, I check on Bethany. Cracking her door open a little more, I peek in. Her sleepy eyes meet mine, a tired smile on her lips.

"Thanks for dinner."

"Of course." She yawns, snuggling into her covers more.

"I have a gig this weekend. I'd like you there."

"Okay."

"Viking and Princess are coming."

"Oh cool."

"Night," I grumble.

"Good night." She sighs, her eyes closing. I can't help but pause and stare for a few seconds before leaving her doorway.

Peeling my clothes off, I leave them on my bedroom floor in my wake. I lie flat on my own bed; it's a California King since I'm six feet four. Regular beds don't work too well for me.

My eyes close and I see Bethany's smirk as she punches Honey. I didn't say it outright, but it was hot as fuck. If she had really been claiming me, I'd have her in my bed right now, rewarding her with my face between those thighs.

When she kissed me, I had to touch them. Every time she puts on a pair of shorts, I want to run my hands up the backs and give them a good smack, leaving a pink handprint behind. Fuck, the things I'd do to her body.

Groaning, my hand finds my semihard cock and I give a few rough pumps. It hardens quickly, precum spilling from the top as I pretend it's her doing it.

"Ummm...Night?" Her voice breaks my thoughts, and my eyes pop open, landing on her flushed cheeks.

"Yeah?" It's gruff, but fuck, five more minutes and I would've been spilling all over myself.

"Can I lay with you?" It's so soft and innocent, I could break down a door with how hard it makes my dick.

"Yeah, come 'ere dollface," I reply and let her scoot under the covers, coming to lie on my chest.

It's going to be one hell of a long night for me. I should just fuck her right here, right now. But I won't. I'm going to let her fall for me before I claim her and finally make her mine.

Sapphire Knight

CHAPTER 16

Live your life by a compass

not a clock.

-Stephan Covey

BETHANY

Watching him play the other night at the bar was insane. I had no idea Nightmare was that talented. Makes me wonder why he ever became a biker in the first place and not a professional drummer. He's at that level, and it's not often you come across someone who is.

"What are you doing?" I ask, pausing in the doorway to the bathroom. He's got a few drops of oil he's rubbing between his palms.

"I'm putting beard oil in my beard." His gaze meets mine while staring into the mirror above the sink. His eyebrow rises like I'm off my rocker.

"Beard oil?"

"Yeah, you know, to make it softer?" His gaze flicks back to the dark hair as he runs his hands over it.

"Hmm," I reply and watch as he smooths it over the long scruff.

Knowing he uses products like that, I have to admit is pretty damn stimulating. Men like him, you think are naturally good-looking, but he works to take care of himself, and that is so attractive in a man.

I caught him in the garage the other morning lifting weights shirtless, and I swear the guy gave me hot flashes. He busted me gawking at him them, too, but I didn't care. Any woman in their right mind would watch muscles like his flex with each lift.

A biker who wears beard oil, lifts weights, plays the drums, and can kiss like the devil himself. Why is it I'm protesting living with him again? Oh right, because he packed my shit up and moved us here without having a real choice in the matter. Doing things like that makes me stabby, no matter how fuckable he may appear.

And let's not mention that he also holds me at night when the dreams haunt me full force. The asshole's not making my life any easier being sweet like that.

"You coming by the club later?" He stands in front of me in the living room on his way out.

"I wasn't planning on it, why?"

"Just checking."

"I need to find a job."

He shrugs. "Not really, but I'm done arguing with you over it."

There's no way in hell I'm letting him pay for my stuff. I won't depend on him any more than he's already caused me too.

"It's not an argument if I want to work."

"Whatever. You could come to the club."

"And do what? Watch one of the whores rub all over you again? That's not my idea of fun."

"She didn't rub on me; she asked if I wanted my cock sucked. I turned her down and then you punched her. Pretty sure the message was clear, and that was a week ago. You're still thinkin' about it?"

"Of course. Women don't let that sort of thing drop."

"You're being a bitch right now, you know that?"

He did not just say that shit to my face. "You better leave before I take a knife to that pretty bike you have parked out front."

He huffs, stuffing his wallet in his pocket.

"And Nightmare?"

"Yeah, B?"

"Next time you call me a bitch or say I'm acting like one?"

He remains stoic, glaring at me.

"You won't be the only one known as Nightmare," I finish and walk toward my bedroom. I'm getting dressed and finding a fucking job if it's the last thing I do today.

Why would he want to know if I'm coming to the club anyhow? It doesn't matter; Princess said she'd watch Mav while I go job hunting, so that's what the plan for the day is.

NIGHTMARE

So moody and for no damn reason, I think as I take my spot at church. Everyone else is already here; I'm running late thanks to Bethany being pissed over old shit.

"Everyone straight?" Viking peers at each of us, waiting for somebody to speak up.

Chaos grumbles, drawing our attention. "Spoke to Cain, he said the charter over there is having a shit time with another club again."

"Iron Fists are back?"

The name rings a bell. Pretty sure that was the club we went on a run to Cali for and torched. We burnt every dirty fucker alive inside too. The club shouldn't be having any issues with the Fists; they should all be dead.

Chaos shrugs. "I don't know if they're back, but they have video of two wearing their colors vandalizing a building next to the compound. They can't pin down a location on them."

"Fuck," Viking mutters. "Ares hasn't called yet, so we'll leave it for now. But...keep your eyes open for them. We killed a lot of those fuckers the last time we chased them down. Doesn't mean we got 'em all, though, and they could be coming for retaliation."

"It's been what, three years?" Sinner blurts.

"Yeah; however, if you think about it in terms of revenge, it's plenty of time for us to be forgetting about them. It's smart. We're not lookin' for them, and they can snuff us out before we get our feet on the ground."

"True. So we just sit back and wait? Not our usual style, brother." I give my two cents.

"I know. I don't like it either, but if we keep watch and wait on 'em, we'll catch them. Hopefully for good this time. I'm sick of these stupid fucks. If we don't have any other business, I'm going to head over to the other club. See if we can get a church session with the other brothers and come up with a more concrete plan. I'm sure Ares is already plotting."

"I'll head over with you."

It's probably not a good idea to be out riding alone if there's someone on the hunt for us. The other brothers agree with me and decide to come along as well, strength in numbers and all. Viking gives Ares a call to see if we can do church with them now versus waiting.

"Appreciate you sitting down with us and having us at your table," Viking grumbles once Ares calls attention to everyone piled into their small room they use for church. It's smaller than ours, but since we wanted to talk, we came to them.

"You're welcome here anytime, brother," Ares replies and glances at each of us. I'm sitting across from Twist, crazy blond fucker covered in more tattoos than myself. Most of the brothers stand, lining the room, as only ten of us can fit around the table. "Now, what's going on?"

"Chaos brought it up that the Iron Fists may have returned."

Collective growls and murmurs scatter amongst the members.

"You heard right. Wasn't gonna drag your members into it unless shit got heavy."

"I'm thinking the bastards may be jonesin' for some retaliation with my crew. Figured it best we hit you up."

Cain sits forward. "You're probably right. We need to fuck 'em up before they hurt anyone like the last time they came through." He glances at Ares as several of the brothers agree with an 'aye.'

My gaze hits Twist briefly, stopping on the scar running along the top of his forehead. He got some of the blow back from the Fists the last time they were in town. Brother had to be transported to the hospital after shrapnel made him flip his bike. That feels like a lifetime ago though.

"We're not here to overstep, Ares. Let us know your plan, and we've got your back." Viking ignores Cain's suggestion, concentrating on the other Prez.

None of us have any issues with Cain, especially myself as his kid plays with mine. Cain and his ol' lady are good people, but this is a discussion held by the Presidents to then be voted on by all of us.

"Your friendship is valuable to this club, we won't forget that or how you've helped in the past," the Prez says to the other, and they clasp hands.

Once enemies, they're now brothers, friends, and each other's full supporter. At one point, I as well as most of the club thought we'd catch hell because we were sure Viking was going to end up killing Ares. They surprised us all by bonding over Princess. There's so much history between us all; we've grown to respect each other a great deal.

"Now," Ares clears his throat, "we've discussed this. We're watching the feeds around the compound and have taken some funds to send the families on vacation, minus a few of us. Avery will stay here along with London to help keep the clubhouse running. London's mom and brother have taken her and Cain's kids out of town, so they're safe."

Of course, those two would be left behind. The Prez's ol' lady along with Cain's. Cain won't let London out of his sight from what I hear, along with those two women being kamikazes. They're almost as bad as Princess and Bethany. The four of them together could seriously cause a shit storm if they wanted to.

"With them gone, we're tryin' to figure out where these jackoffs are stayin'. Once we find out, we're blowing them sky high. Fuck the dumb shit; I'm done with them existin'."

"That sounds all good, except, what if this isn't all of them?" Blaze grumbles, sitting next to Viking. "We've all heard how this club has chapters in Texas and Cali and that some of the compounds can't be found."

"We torched their south Texas or Mexican border club years back," 2 Piece answers. Not only is he a club officer; he's Ares' property. Yes, you heard that correctly. Ares has an ol' lady and an ol' man. "Then the Nomads torched the Cali club," he finishes, and I nod, confirming his explanation. 2 Piece actually rode with us on that hit. He's cool in my book, true to his position and loyal to the club.

Viking sips some whiskey from his flask, his eyes shooting to Spider. "Spidey, can you do some tech shit and find out if these fuckers have been popping up anywhere else?" He rode back in last night and couldn't have timed it any better.

"Yeah, I can, uh, run the club's video against a facial recognition program I have that's linked into the justice monitoring system via stateside."

"Whatever the fuck you just said, do it." Viking nods, and a few of us chuckle. We have no idea what the hell Spider is talking about half the time, but it sounds good. He's one smart fucker, probably bordering on genius. No idea what someone with his head is doing riding with a bunch of outlaws.

Pulling a smoke free, Ares watches as I light it up, swallowing and staring longingly. We've all heard the stories how Avery has his nuts in a vice when it comes to him smoking.

"Pass me a smoke, lad." Scot holds his hand out, and I dig my pack back out, handing it over and gesturing for him to pass it around. None of these idiots thought to bring their own, just their drinks. Everybody started staring at me like a fucking kicked puppy when I flicked open my zippo. May as well share, so they stop their silent whining.

Once everyone's had some nicotine hit their system, the talk continues, and a plan formulates. My girl and kid will be fine, as no one knows about them. Princess lives with Viking and Odin, so she'll be straight as well. Bronx will be posted up at the bar with Scot's ol' lady to offer her some protection in case the Fists stop through at the bar. I'll keep Bethany and Maverick safe, and if shit hits the fan, I can move them to my room in the club for the time being.

Extending my legs, I roll my ankle around as much as I can in my heavy riding boots. My leg is achy today. Not sure why, but I may need to adjust the leg weights or something. I want it strong but not reinjured. Bad enough it'll never look the same, but it hurts a lot of the time, too. Nothing a decent double shot of Jack can't fix, though.

Church comes to an end, and we head back to our clubhouse after sharing a drink with the original Oath Keepers.

CHAPTER 17

I hope to arrive to my death,

late, in love, and a little drunk.

-Atticus

BETHANY

After job hunting, I decide to say screw it and stop by the compound. Nightmare obviously wanted me here for some reason. I don't know why, but whatever, guess we'll find out.

Heading into the clubhouse, I see him instantly. How can I not? Anytime he's in the vicinity, I'm immediately drawn to him. He calls to me on a deeper level, as if his soul is an old friend of mine.

Honey has her hand wrapped around his bicep, and it's all I can take. Princess was right about it sparking jealousy inside me. I'm not a jealous person either, but Nightmare is my hard limit. No one needs to touch him like she's doing.

Stopping, I decide it's best to just leave, rather than hit her again. I don't know if he enjoys her attention and pretends otherwise, but fuck that. I don't have time for bullshit, especially when I already have enough grief from him.

I'm a grown-ass woman, and while I like to tangle, I won't put up with club crap. I'm not an ol' lady; I don't have dibs on him, even if it feels as if I should. In reality, he's not mine. He never was, and he probably never will be.

I barely poked my head in, and, thankfully, no one noticed me. I make my way back to the parking lot full of bikes and my car. It stands out like a neon sign amongst the beautifully painted motorcycles. Especially Nightmare's. I've always loved the glossy black finish. It's humongous up close, definitely a bike fit for a big man. The best word to describe Night would be imposing, and his bike, no doubt, fits that description as well.

My fingertips trail over his seat, the same place I sat on when he took me with him to see him play at Shorty's. God, I loved watching him beat on those drums. It was practically sinful, his hair going in every direction, his biceps flexing as sweat beaded on his forehead. *Yum.*

My anger ignites again as I glance at the carefully airbrushed sandman on the tank. It's creepy as fuck and fits his name perfectly. He's the shit that nightmares are made of if you piss him off in the wrong way.

I made a promise that he wouldn't be the only one around here known as a Nightmare if he crossed me. My actual words were him calling me or insinuating that I was being a bitch, but I'd say this instance counts. It's the perfect time to teach the man a lesson.

I giggle to myself. It's probably more like a cackle, a crazy one, but who's paying attention at this point. My mind's made up. It's time to play with my food, my meal being Nightmare.

Pulling my keys free from my purse, I open the small pocket knife I keep on my keyring and bend toward his back tire where no one can see me. Finding the softest spot on the back tire, I press the blade into the thick rubber. It's no easy feat, but I get it with some pressure. It won't go flat immediately with the clean slice, but it'll do the trick with a little time.

Wearing an evil grin, I let out a deep breath. That felt freaking great! Not one to let my handy work go unnoticed, I head for the beautiful white airbrush design and scrape a large *B*right in the middle of the sandman.

Fucking piss me off bastard biker, and I'll show you what crazy is. I could never be his ol' lady because of shit like this. I'd end up slitting a hoe's throat for touching him; I'm not patient like Princess is. She gets club life; she belongs here. Me, well, he'd probably strangle me by the time Maverick turned ten years old.

I found a job. It's nothing special, but it'll do. Obviously, with my little tantrum here, I'll need it, too. He'll want me to pay to have his shit fixed no doubt, but it won't happen. At least this way he should be pissed enough to make me move out, which is the end goal after all.

Sucks he's so damn good-looking and enticing, makes it harder to be evil toward him. I would've loved it if we could work things out, but he hates me for keeping our son from him. I can't blame him for feeling that way, but I refuse to be around him twenty-four hours a day, in his arms if he can't forgive me.

I can hear the air slowly escaping the tire. The sound's barely there, and if he leaves soon, he won't notice it right away more than likely. I'd think he'd see the gash in his tank first off and then the tire would be the little kicker following up my handiwork.

Ugh, I hope he doesn't try riding it like this though. While I want to piss him off and screw with him, I don't want him to wreck and seriously injure himself. He's been a decent dad to Mav so far...No, he's been a great father to our son. I'm a bitch, but he already knows that. He mentioned it earlier. Perhaps I should carve *bitch* on the other side.

Nah, that may be pushing it. I want him furious, not feeling lethal.

One last glance at my special surprise, and I make the trek back to my car, grinning the entire way.

Welcome to crazy town motherfucker. Next time you'll remember why I punched the slut in the first place.

For you.

208

NIGHTMARE

We head out to the parking lot; half of the brothers are planning to hit up Scot's ol' ladies bar. I'm done, ready to go have dinner with my family, especially after brushing Honey off all damn afternoon. It seems as if she's more persistent now that Bethany's come around and let her presence be known.

It's getting old fast. I haven't given her any reason to believe I'd be interested. It's fucking annoying. I don't fuck club pussy—never have, never will. They all know this, but a new bitch shows up, and it's like everyone forgets to leave me the hell alone in the process. Maybe my glare isn't as menacing now that I'm getting older. Back in the day, one nasty look would send a chick running scared.

My rear tire looks a bit low. I may need to pull it over to the garage and top it off with the compressor before hitting the highway. A low tire and some gravel can screw up anyone, even seasoned riders. We need to be extra careful and prepared with the talk of the Iron Fists being in town as well. Last thing we want is to be caught unprepared by some dickwads with an axe to grind.

"Daaaaaamn." Saint laughs and points at my tank, clearly amused by something.

"The fuck?" I grit, pulling a smoke free and lighting it. Fucker's losing it, I know it. Sinner needs to reel his homeboy's shit in.

"You pissed someone off, brother." Sinner chuckles, shaking his head, and I finally come to stand beside them.

Sure as hell my tank is scratched up—deeply. This was no accidental brush up or dip from someone. This was intentional and caused some serious damage. Taking a deep breath, I run my hand over the deep indentions. My scarred palm sits on the warm metal, and it hits me.

It's a motherfuckin' B.

"Motherfuckin' woman, Jesus Christ. I'm gonna strangle her ass for this."

"You need help taking care of whoever did this?" Saint offers, and I shake my head. I'll smack her ass cherry red for pulling something this ballsy.

"Nah. I know exactly who did this. I can handle her on my own."

Sinner's eyes widen. "Shit, no way, it was Bethany? You pissed her off pretty bad for that one, huh?" His charcoal irises glance to Saint, an amused grin painted amongst the dark scruff overtaking his jaw.

"I didn't do shit to her. Bitch is fucking crazy in the head. She's gonna put me on my death bed with her antics if she keeps it up."

There's nothing I can do besides order a new tire to be delivered because I'd bet my left nut that's her doing as well. I'm sure there's a hole somewhere if I look close enough; hell, maybe one in the front, too. Glad we came out pretty early; would've been bad if it was at night and I didn't notice right away.

Daydream

How she came up with this in the first place is beyond me. You'd think I made her life hell with the torture she put my bike through.

If it were anyone other than her, I'd be hunting them down for retribution. You don't mess with a man's bike. It's like rule number one in this lifestyle. I need to call Spin at the other club, too, and see if he and Twist can repaint and then airbrush my tank this week. This blows and not in a good way.

Looks like I'm borrowing Scot's truck again. I hope for B's sake she's not home, 'cause this is going to take more than the drive home for me to calm my shit. She has some serious explaining to do, and she's either sorting it out to be fixed, or she's paying me in pussy. Whatever it is, she better get on board, because she crossed a fucking line. *Again.*

I end up stopping for gas for Scot's truck and then driving around for an hour trying to think and cool off. Cooling down is not my usual behavior. Normally, I'd find the person and make them pay in however I saw fit, but, this time, it's different.

I don't want to do something that she won't be able to forgive me for. Why I care, I don't know. Do I have feelings for her? Of course, I do. I had a soft spot from the moment I pulled her onto my lap in that stupid bar.

She was lit up on alcohol and painkillers, but that's not what I saw when I looked at her. I saw someone who was damaged like me, yet she was beautiful. Somehow, she'd survived and was put in my path. Then I lost her and thought maybe I was being an idiot.

Clearly, I wasn't since she's the mother of my child. I don't care what anyone says, what anyone tries to make you believe, but when a woman has your child, she automatically carves out a piece of you. I could hate her with every breath I have, but, in the end, she carried and gave birth to my son. For that alone, I'll owe her forever.

I should despise her for what she's done, but after seeing how good she is to Maverick, I can't. I ought to, I know it, but I don't. Truth is, I want her, and as each day passes us, my anger from her deceit dissipates, and my hunger to have her grows.

I've never wanted a woman so badly in my life like I do her, and especially after pulling something crazy like she did today. It makes me want to fuck her until she begs for my forgiveness. I want her to plead with me to make her mine, so I don't look like the weak one in this. When it boils down to it, I am. I'd probably do anything she asked, and that's so goddamn scary, to let someone own you like that.

Pulling up to my house, it all looks the same. Well, the same since she and Mav have arrived. The front porch light shines brightly, as does the one over the garage. The blinds are closed, but I can see Bethany left the kitchen light on over the sink, and I'd bet there's a plate full of whatever she cooked waiting for me in the microwave, too.

It's something I never had growing up or throughout my life—consistency and care. My father's wives never did it; that's for sure. Hell, they never had a chance to. Life was probably terrifying living with a man whose moods were constantly swinging from one side to the other. It was rough for me being his son, can't imagine having to be married to the bastard.

I don't want to be that way with Bethany. I know I'm a bit moody and quiet, but that's just who I am. I never want her to fear for her safety when it comes to me. Her sanity maybe, since she drives me just as crazy it seems.

I bypass the kitchen, going straight for the room she's taken over since moving in. She belongs in my bedroom with me, but we haven't hit that level yet. She wants her space, and I'm attempting to give it to her.

Maverick ought to be knocked out by now, so he shouldn't hear shouting if there turns out to be any. While arguing may be a natural part of a relationship, I don't want my kid witnessing his mom and me going at each other. Her actions today tell me she wants a fight.

Pushing the door open, Bethany's gaze meets mine, and instantly her eyes widen. She knows she fucked up. I probably look like an angry bear storming in while she's in her normal nighttime attire. The first time I saw her wearing only her cami shirt with no bra and a pair of panties, I thought my dick was going to pop out of my pants on its own accord.

She's already beautiful—the kind of classic beauty that she thinks makes her look plain. She's nowhere near ordinary, she's perfect. Pair that with barely any clothes and it's enough to tongue-tie me, making me think of other things I want to do with her. Not right now, though. I need to get my point across.

"You fucked up," I growl, grabbing her by her biceps and slamming her onto her back against the bed.

Grabbing at my hands, she sputters, "Please, I'm sorry, I know, okay?"

Taking her wrists into one of my palms, I grip them above her head. Then wrap my other around her neck just tight enough to make her nervous, and I bring my nose to hers. "You don't touch a man's bike. That kind of crazy ain't cute dollface," I growl. It's hard to be pissed when my body's laying over hers on top of a bed. I can feel her curves in all the right places.

"Night, I can't breathe." She sucks in a breath through her lips.

"Bullshit." I flex my fingers tighter, and she sputters again. "See, you got breathing room." My lips nearly touch hers as I peer into her shocked irises. "You owe me, Bethany. How you gonna repay me for this little tantrum of yours?"

"I, uh..."

My mouth whispers over her lips, "You finally gonna give up that pussy, baby?"

"You want it?" she replies breathily, making my heart stutter.

"Fuck yes."

"Good, keep wanting it. You won't be touching it anytime soon."

"Fucking bitch." My nostrils flare, and she leans up, quick enough to bite my bottom lip savagely. "Shit!" I pull back as the coppery taste of blood overtakes my tongue. "I should bruise your ass for that one."

"You won't, not until I give in, and right now, it's not happening. And don't call me bitch, bastard."

Grumbling, I push off the bed, releasing her as I stand and adjust myself. The woman's going to be the

214

goddamn death of me. "You have to give me something. You fucked my shit up."

"Fine." She stands, coming chest to chest with me. "You want something?"

I watch her. She could be baiting me. This is Bethany we're talking about. She's not like other women; she likes to keep me on my toes. I'm always guessing when it comes to her.

B licks her lips and drops to her knees. Seeing her below me like that has me awestruck. She's breathtaking.

Quickly she unbuckles my belt and unsnaps my jeans, letting the zipper down. My cock is throbbing with need, wanting her to touch and feel me everywhere. It's been too long since I've been with a woman. Having her here, like this has me damn near jittery with excitement.

"Still a boxer brief man, I see," she states, pushing my pants and underwear down my thighs.

I mutter a reply, but it comes out more as jibber-jabber. She probably didn't understand me; hell, *I* don't even know what I said. All that matters right now is her hand gripping on to my cock like she's about to downshift into second gear or some shit. It's tight and feels magnificent.

"Fuck," I gasp, with her tongue coming to lick my tip like a lollipop.

"Oh, Nightmare, you still taste good, too." Bethany winks up at me, and my stomach tightens with lust. I want to taste her, too, feel her against me.

"Let me bury my cock in you."

"Mmm, no." The tip of my dick sinks between her plump lips before she pulls back and finishes. "I won't be that easy for you, again," she promises and then sucks my cock all the way to the back of her throat.

I'd probably offer her a ring at a moment like this if I knew it would sway her, but it won't. Bethany's never been the marrying type. She'll be loyal for life, I can tell, but she doesn't need a man's last name to do so. She reminds me of myself in so many ways. Maybe that's why I've wanted her so badly from the start.

Her head bobs and she swirls her tongue as she draws backward. I'm damn near to the point I should probably say a prayer thanking whatever being is responsible for creating her. That mouth of hers is torture in the best and worst of ways when it comes to me.

"You weren't easy. I never gave you a choice; I was having you and we had fun." Groaning, my hands tangle in her brunette locks. "Fuck, you're good at that, baby."

"Say my name."

"Huh?"

Her eyes look up, stopping on my own. "I said, 'say my name,' Nightmare. Who am I? Who's sucking your cock right now?"

"Bethany." It leaves my mouth in a whoosh as her lips sink back over my length. I have to hand it to her; the bossy shit turns me on like no other. "Suck my cock, Bethany," I demand, and her teeth graze over my sensitive skin, causing my nuts to tingle, building anticipation.

Daydream

She pauses, licking the tip in short, quick strokes and prickly sensations overtake the arches of my feet as amazing sensations shoot in every direction throughout my body. One powerful twist around my cock from both of her hands at the same time while she draws me inside her warm, wet mouth and I'm gone. My feet flex inside my motorcycle boots, my leg achy from balancing. Next, my hands that're already gripping her hair, close into fists, pulling and groaning as my mind fades into pure bliss and my cum shoots down her welcoming throat.

Pump after pump she swallows what I give her, and for the first time since she's arrived, it's like I can think clearly again. The fog she's had me in finally begins to thin, and everything's not angry or fuzzy. I'm here, in this moment, with her.

"Are you still mad?" she mutters, climbing to her feet. She wipes over her lips and I swallow thickly at the sight. I don't think I could ever get enough when it comes to her.

Shaking my head, I fix my pants. "Nah, but what knife did you use to cut my tire?"

"It's ummm...the one on my keyring." She gestures to the dresser and then goes and gets her keys. Holding her palm out in front of me, I lift them up, finding the small pocket knife. It's the definition of cute to a chick. To me, it looks like something I would've had when I was six.

"Dollface, let me get you a knife, yeah?" I remove her *knife* which would be considered a nail cleaner to me and hand her the keys. B nods, her stare curious.

She follows me to my room, where I go to my closet to retrieve an actual knife. It's the type she

217

should be carrying for safety or whatever it is she uses it for. Holding out the dark purple handle, she takes it from me.

"Wow, a switchblade?" She palms it in one hand, looking it over, then switches to the other hand, weighing it.

"Yeah, baby, you need something better than that scrap of metal you had on your key ring. You're lucky it didn't break in my tire and cut your damn hand. I'd have been more pissed havin' to call up the doc because you needed stitched up," I mutter, and she rewards me with a bright smile. "What?" She's not going to fight me on it?

"Nothing, just...thank you for this." She presses the lever with her finger—with a bright blue polished nail—and the blade shoots out. My breath falters a bit like some sort of candy-ass.

"Now, be careful with that shit."

"I will." She grins, sheathing the blade again. She twists around, heading for her room.

"Where are you going?"

"To bed! Dinner's in the microwave," the troublemaker calls behind her like I should already know.

I can't believe she didn't fight me on the knife. The downfall to that is if she gets pissed again, she can really screw up some shit with it. Hopefully, it's not my bike that takes the heat again...or me, for that matter.

CHAPTER 18

Shit's gettin' real.

Saddle up and hold on.

A week has passed in pretty much a blur. Bethany started a new job that I wasn't happy about, but on the plus side, it's close to the house. She only works during the day, too, so that's an advantage.

I like what consists of family time that we get together even if I piss her off half of the time. She picks up Maverick from Princess and heads home, and then I show up sometime later. We've began our first routine it seems.

It's crazy how much things change when you have a woman and a kid in your life. I no longer want to sit at the club, drinking and bullshitting with my brothers. I'd rather be home with them. Sure, I enjoy my time at the club, but I also enjoy my time with her and Maverick, too.

Before, if I wasn't working out or fixing up a bike, I would go a little stir-crazy at home alone. I've always been sort of a loner, but after being around my brothers for so long, I've grown used to them and their company. Having B and Mav at the house has taken away the quiet. They're always doing something, too, whether it's watching TV, listening to music, or Maverick's busy building some sort of fort in the living room.

Pulling my bike up beside her car, I park the freshly-painted beauty and make my way up the small walkway. That's another thing she's done; she's planted flowers. Never gave two shits about that sort of thing before, but I like them, too.

The small touches make the place seem homier rather than just a crash pad. It's got me thinking about painting the trim and front door as well. The chick is domesticating my ass just by bringing plants around. Ruger would love to find that out and give me some shit over it, I'd bet.

Heading up the walkway, I immediately catch sight that the main door isn't shut all the way, which has me curious. I wonder if Maverick was screwing with it. B asked me to install a chain lock up high, and I haven't done it yet.

Seeing the door cracked, though, I'll make sure and get to it this weekend. The last thing I want is our kid outside when no one is watching him. He's smart, but he's no angel, I've come to discover.

Entering quietly, I hear her. It sounds almost like she's pleading with someone not to hurt her son. *Our son.* I don't have any clue what the fuck's going down, so I draw my blade free from my pants. Flicking the large, heavy blade open, I creep stealthily through the entryway. They're in the living room which throws me in the middle of the scene immediately.

Some fucker in an Iron Fists cut is in my living room, holding a gun at Bethany, who's standing in front of my son protectively. He notices me immediately, switching tactics. He pulls her in front of his body and aims his weapon toward me.

"Get over to where I can see you, Oath Keeper," he hisses, and his teeth are black, from a bad Meth habit if I had to guess.

Doing as he says, I hold my palms out to my sides. I keep a solid grip on my blade with my thumb, but act as if I don't want any trouble. My gaze is surprised like he has one up on me.

I watch in utter amazement as Bethany holds her keys tightly in her palm, keeping it together. She must've been coming home from her new job when this asshole saw her and followed her and Maverick home. I have to give her major props for staying strong and protecting our child while I wasn't here.

"Momma?" My son steps forward and Bethany sputters.

"No, no, no buddy." She holds her free hand out in a stop motion. "You stay over there and hold onto that puppy for Mommy. I don't want you coming over here or I could get hurt."

"Ummm...hurt?" His little worried gaze takes in the scene before him as he holds the sleeping puppy.

"Yes, I don't want any owies, so sit with the puppy; he needs you to cuddle him while he sleeps."

He sighs and slowly sits with the dog, watching everything unfold. I don't think he buys it completely, but he's smart so he stays where he is.

"Who the fuck are *you*? Why are you in my house?" I grumble toward the man I'll be killing shortly. He'll be lucky if I don't string him up and torture him for pulling this little stunt with my family.

"I'm Shadow. And your fucking club killed my older brother."

"Who was your brother?"

At this rate, it could be anyone. We've had our fair share of killing shitbags throughout the club. I'm guessing it was an Iron Fist we torched, as his cut advertises he's affiliated with the same club. None of it matters anyhow; I'm only concerned with keeping him talking.

"Ghost was my brother. Someone from your club killed him," he repeats.

I know exactly who it was, too—Twist and Ares. I remember the exact day, as a matter of fact. They'd called us over for a beer to fill us in on what went down that afternoon. I was still a Nomad at the time.

"I'm coming to kill each one of you." As soon as he finishes, he aims and fires his Glock at me, gripping the back of Bethany's neck tightly with his free hand. Her cringe, has me wanting to extract what teeth he has one by one, so he can feel my wrath for laying his filthy hands on her.

The kick causes the shot to go wide and the bullet hits me in the shoulder. It stings, but that's not what hurts. It's the screams leaving my girl and my son that wind me. He just signed his death certificate. *Bye-bye motherfucker.*

Shaking it off, I spread my feet and grit through the burning sensation. I've been attacked by a motherfuckin' lion; a bullet won't drop me. Not today, at least. I have to protect my family, and I'll do it with everything in me.

"Again, why are you doing this to me and my family?" I need to distract him enough to get his hand away from Bethany's throat, so I can get to him without her getting hurt badly.

Thank God Maverick is a good kid and listens to his mom telling him to stay away from her. He clutches the puppy to his chest as tears roll down his cheeks, confused and scared by what's happening in his own home. I want to kill this asshole for touching Bethany already, but the fact he's making my kid cry, it makes me want to filet him—slowly. I swear if I don't get to finish him outright, I'll burn plastic until it melts into scalding hot liquid then I'll coat his flesh in it and peel him like a goddamn orange. This motherfucker won't know what pain is until I get a turn at him.

B's eyes flick to Mav again, full of concern, I know she's torn on what to do. He sits only a few feet away from the hell happening in our living room. Hell, I want to grab him and take him someplace safe, but I know I can save them both.

This dipshit, Shadow, didn't come prepared. He was expecting to have access to Bethany without any interference and came alone. It was a dumb mistake on his part.

I told dollface before that you never mess with a man's bike. The other two rules that go along with that are: You never fuck with a man's club, and by all means, you never touch a man's property, so you better be prepared if you do. What comes after screwing with those three things is retaliation, revenge, and murder. I cannot wait to get my hands on him, 'cause I will end him.

She takes a deep breath, and I read her before it even happens. She releases the switchblade, nervously glancing at me, and I nod. *Do it baby. I got you.*

It feels as if it happens in slow motion. Her hand jerks upward, taking assface off guard as she drives the blade into his thigh with everything she's got. He yells, releasing her in shock, and she dives for Maverick. I've never been so proud of her.

In the same breath, I jump for Shadow, bringing my own blade to his throat and ripping it across. Bethany holds our son and the puppy to her chest, covering Maverick's eyes as she watches. Blood showers out from the wound, coating my clothes and the floor beneath my feet.

Flicking my head to the side, Bethany hops around the mess heading for the other room. She doesn't need to see all of this; I wish she hadn't witnessed any of it. Watching the man bleed out below me, I wait until I know he's completely gone before I check on my family.

"You okay?" I mutter, pausing in the doorway.

"We will be." She holds Maverick to her still, sitting on the edge of his bed as the puppy noses a few of my son's toys lying around his room.

"You can come out now."

"I can't let him see that out there. And you need to change."

Glancing down, I see I'm coated in blood spray. "I'll be right back."

I stuff the ruined clothes in a trash bag, put a fresh set on and scrub some of the blood from my hands and arms so I don't freak them out. Then check on Shadow again; he's still dead, so I make my way back to the bedroom.

"Better?"

"Yes, thanks and thank you for what you did in there."

"Of course. I'll always protect you in any way that I can. It didn't freak you out though?"

"Well, yes it did, but you had to do it. That man was going to kill us, and you saved us."

"It was you, Bethany. You did the right thing with that knife; I couldn't have planned it better myself."

"The scariest part of all," she whispers, meeting my gaze, "is that I liked it. I enjoyed every second of watching you slice that guy's throat."

I flick my eyes to my son, and bring them back to hers. "It's because you knew you were safe by me doing it, that's all. Don't worry about nothing, babe."

She nods, taking a deep breath. "I need to pack."

"What? Why?"

"Because, we can't stay here with *him* laying out there in the living room. It's bad enough that Maverick saw as much as he did. I can't keep our son here with the house like this."

"Oh, yeah, I get it. I have a room at the club we can stay at for a few nights until this is all cleaned up."

"Okay, I can get us a couple days' worth of clothes."

"The carpet's no good though. It'll have to come out, most likely the whole room. How about wood floors? Unless you have something specific you'd like."

"You are seriously talking to me about flooring right now?"

"I mean, it'll have to go. It sucks. I liked that carpet too, but—"

"Oh my God! You're going over flooring options with me right now!"

"Well, it's your house, too; I want you to have what you like," I reason, and she bursts into a fit of giggles. It's a beautiful sound and makes me grin, even though I don't know why she's laughing right now.

"Jesus. Okay, Night. How about we go with a dark walnut color?"

"Walnut? Like a tree or nut you buy from the store?"

"Yes, if you go to a floor or hardware store they should have it, and it'll look nice with the furniture."

"Sounds good. You'll need to drive to the clubhouse."

"Without you?"

"I'll be behind you in case anyone else is waiting or tries to follow."

"Okay, just be careful, please. I don't know how you can ride like that." She gestures to my shoulder.

"You gettin' soft on me, Daydream?"

"Maybe just a little," she admits and my thumb grazes her cheek. She's so goddamn stunning, even after all the bullshit she went through today. She shouldn't have to deal with any club blowback, but she got caught up in it regardless.

"I need to text Vike, and then we need to head out," I grumble, pulling my phone out. My adrenaline's pumping too thick right now that the pain in my shoulder hasn't hit me full force yet. I'm not looking forward to when it does, either.

Me: My crib was infested when I got here.

Viking: Bet. I'll get my ol' lady, you should come back.

Me: On our way.

Viking: Be safe

Taking a deep breath, I pull up Chaos next, texting everyone in code.

Me: I need your help with a remodel. Grab Spider and head to my place.

Chaos: Will do.

Me: I'll meet you there shortly.

Chaos: No problem.

"Come on baby, grab Maverick. I'll get the dog and your bags. Chaos and Spider are on their way."

"Will they be okay with..." She points to the other room, and I chuckle. If she only knew just how okay any of the brothers would be, she may lose her shit.

"Yeah, they'll be straight. They'll help me clean up and put the new floor in."

"Okay, make sure you order pizza or something for them."

I chuckle again, shaking my head. There's a dead body in the other room and she's worried about feeding company. And it's not normal company either; these are my brothers who are coming over to help me dispose of a body.

She's definitely a keeper.

We load up, and in no time we're on our way to the club. I can't stop thinking that one of the best decisions I ever made was giving my woman a knife.

CHAPTER 19

I love the 3 am version of people.

Vulnerable. Honest. Real.

BETHANY

"Wait, how did he get into the house? Was he waiting behind you or something?" Princess gapes, asking me a zillion questions about what just went down with Shadow.

"Not exactly. When I first got home, my hands were full, and I was too busy worrying about putting the puppy outside that I didn't lock the door behind me. We let the dog out, came back inside, and Shadow was there waiting for us."

"Fucking creepy." She shudders.

"I know, Prissy, trust me. I wanted to freak out so badly, but was trying to keep it together in front of Maverick."

"You were so lucky Nightmare came home earlier than expected. Who knows what could've happened to you guys if he'd been running late."

"I know, I was thinking the same thing. Luckily, he had to pick up his bike from Spin and was close to the house so decided to come home. To think, if I'd never slashed his motorcycle up, there's a chance we could be dead right now."

"Well, your temper definitely paid off this time. I'm so glad you all are all right."

"God, me too, lady. I hope this isn't something Maverick will remember as he gets older. Nightmare literally slashed the guy's throat in the middle of the living room. With the blood everywhere and Shadow shooting Night in the shoulder, it was gruesome and scary. I can only imagine how he must be feeling right now."

"I know what you mean, babe; the stuff that went down with me in the bar a few years back was pretty crazy, too. We're lucky to have strong men in our lives."

I nod. It's true. If it'd been some "Joe Schmo" down the road, he'd have pissed his pants in fear—not killed the guy. I always believed Nightmare was sort of a badass, but he's really one bad mamma jamma. I witnessed him kick ass with my own two eyes.

"I'm sure Maverick will replace those images of his dad. He's so small now; hopefully, he'll believe it was a dream or something."

"Fingers crossed," I mumble, thinking about how young I was when my dad began hurting me. I have my own demons and know just how daunting dreams can be inflicted by true events.

"Viking flipped his shit when he got Night's text. He had Odin and Torch come get me from the house in case anyone was lurking around the property. When something like this goes down, it usually happens in more than one place, sort of like a distraction. The club is livid. They'll find these guys."

"Good. Is it bad that I hope they seriously hurt them or even kill them? I feel so guilty saying that, but after meeting Shadow...well, I have to think of my own family."

"No, I agree with you. And to be honest, they won't be turning up again after the club finds them. A threat to family is like a cardinal rule when it comes to these guys. Took me being the Prez's ol' lady to realize that and how important we were to my own father growing up. I really had no clue just how much the club protects its own."

"But we don't belong to the club. I'm not Nightmare's ol' lady."

"No, maybe not, but you are his family. Maverick is his son and you mean something to him. That means a lot to the brothers."

"Do I, though?"

"Yes, B; everyone knows it," she reassures me, her statement full of finality making me believe her.

"So, what now?"

"Now, we settle in, maybe get some dinner going because the guys will get hungry. They'll take care of everything else."

"Just like that? You sit back and let them?"

"Yes. This is their club. While we're a part of it, they run things in this lifestyle. We show them support and love them fiercely. In return, they do the same for us."

Taking a deep breath, I nod and send her a smile. "Then lead me to the kitchen. I need something to do, preferably with chocolate involved."

She returns my smile. "Follow me, this kitchen setup is perfect for cooking a ton of food."

NIGHTMARE

"Spidey and Chaos should be there already," Viking mutters, busily texting someone. "Your shirt's soaked. 2 Piece is already here waiting in case any of you need medical care. Now that I see you were shot, I'm glad I'd called him after all."

"I'm fine. It was just a shoulder graze. Nothing I can't handle."

"Look, I don't give a fuck if you're fine. You have a kid and a woman now, suck it the fuck up and get stitched up," he glowers and I roll my eyes like a petulant child. Last thing I feel like doing is having 2 poking around my shoulder with a damn needle.

"Fine, fuck it. 2 Piece?" I gesture, and he brings his glass and a small tote with him.

"Where did it hit you?" he questions, eyes raking over me quickly.

"My shoulder." I yank my shirt over my head. It's pretty bloody, and I just changed before we left. Good thing my shirt's black. It sucks ass trying to get blood out of clothes.

"Damn." He cringes and pulls a few bottles and other supplies from his bag. "It went straight through, luckily. You'll be tender here for some time, though, and the shoulder's an easy spot to rip stiches out for us. Careful riding, fighting, lifting, fucking, that sort of stuff."

"So, basically, everything then." Grumbling, I get situated. Fucker should've gone to medical school, not joined a biker club. "Appreciate you fixing me up," I acknowledge and he waves me off, getting to work. Bad enough he had to ride over here with shit hitting the fan.

I turn back to Viking, ignoring the pain from 2 Piece cleaning and digging into my flesh while he sews my wound up. "I told Bethany that Chaos and Spider needed to come by to help me redo the floors."

"Good. You having them use that deep pit out back of your place to burn the body?"

"Yeah. I figured they'd look him over for any more information as well. Spider can snap a pic for the photo search he's been doing this week too. May help us find some more answers."

"Bet. I'm sorry this happened to your family, brother, but it may end up being a blessing in disguise."

"I thought the same thing, actually. We need to find these motherfuckers and snuff them all out. Put an end to whatever future plans they may be up to."

"Agreed. I'm talkin' to Ares right now, working on keepin' him up to speed."

"'Kay. If you're straight here, then I'm heading back to my place to help them clean up."

2 Piece grabs the bloody gauze and other supplies, heading for the bathroom and I pull my shirt back on. The shoulder area's a bit stiff from the blood drying, but it'll do for now. I can grab another back at the house and burn all my bloody clothes with Shadow's body. No body, no blood, no evidence, no murder is the way I see it. That motto hasn't let me down yet.

"We've got it handled. If I find out anything, I'll hit you up. You three keep a lookout for any more joiners coming to the party late, and hit me back if you see any Iron Fists period. I'll see about getting the other club here by the time y'all are back for church."

I nod and bump his knuckles. I know he'll make sure Bethany and Maverick are safe here while I go take care of business. I hate leaving them at all after what they just went through. At least B has Princess here to help her process it all. Probably no one better for that job anyhow.

Shadow coming around shakes everything up. It went from us looking out for the other club to a direct threat against us as well. The other club, they aren't as ... how do I put it? Not as savage as we are. I think that's the best way to explain them.

Daydream

They're hard, sure, but we were Nomads before turning over our patch to a home charter. We dealt with the worst of the worst and prospered. That Nomad brand of crazy still pumps through our veins, and this is giving us a prime excuse to cash in on it.

Before I leave, I search Bethany out. She needs to realize that not only was Shadow a game changer for the club, he was for me as well. I'm done fooling with her. I flat out want her. Yes, she fucked up, and, yes, it will forever be in my mind, but I'm moving past it. I'm putting what matters most in perspective—her and my son. Nothing is more important to me than the two of them.

"I'm taking off." I find her and Princess in the midst of a huge mess in the kitchen. I can't help but grin, thinking about how this'll piss the club sluts off something fierce having to do cleanup duty. I know Princess, though, and she'll give zero fucks. My girl need P right now to show her how to cope; I'm glad she has her.

"You have to go?" Her gaze flicks to the floor, and I can tell she's biting the inside of her cheek. She's still shook up. Can't say I blame her.

Grabbing her forearm lightly, I tug her in my direction. "Gotta go and make sure no more idiots are lurking around. You know how I am about you having bad dreams about shit. Figure I'll squash them now and you'll sleep like a baby." Winking, I bring her against my chest.

It's true. Her nightmares drive me up the fucking wall. If I hear her having one, I've started to automatically carry her to my bed so they stop and she sleeps. I don't want this giving her more shit at night as well.

"I know. I really don't want you caught riding alone though."

"One of them couldn't handle me with you in the middle of it. Trust me, B; they damn sure can't handle me alone."

She sighs, still worried, and I pull her closer until her chest is flush against mine and my arms are around her securely. "I'll be fine, Daydream," I utter as I bend down until her lips are to mine.

My hand tangles in her long, dark, chocolate-colored hair and my tongue glides over hers tenderly. The kiss is full of so many feelings I've been holding back, hiding away inside. If I could tell her with merely a kiss just how I feel about her, I would. I'm not sure she'll get it, but I do my damndest anyhow.

Her palm lands on my chest, bunching my T-shirt fabric in her hands as she gives it back just as well as she takes it. I wish the lip lock was under different circumstances and I wasn't about to leave. If anything, the kiss is good motivation to take care of business quickly and get back to her.

"Behave," I murmur, as I pull away. My toes tingle as I remember what her mouth's capable of doing.

She grins as I bump my nose against hers gently, and then I'm out the door, in pissed-off biker mode, ready to fuck up some Fists, if needed.

Thankfully, cleanup went quick, and we made it back to the club in one piece. Having to lift shit with my shoulder sucked, but I got through it. There's nothing more relaxing than lighting a body on fire—other than sex. To me anyhow. I relish in that shit. It can't just be anyone, either. It has to be a piece of shit whose flesh gets melted off by my hands for it to do the trick.

"This crazy goin' on better not be giving you ideas to go Nomad again."

Grinning at Viking, I shake my head. "Nah, you'd miss me too much."

"Not to sound like a bitch, but yeah, I would actually. When we were Nomad, you and Ex were the two brothers I trusted the most. You didn't run your mouths and you owned your shit. I want to be surrounded by that in my own club. I have Princess now; I can't have a Nomad charter."

"I get it, and you don't have to worry about me either. I have Bethany and Mav now. No way I'm leaving them. Truthfully, though, if they weren't around, I'd love to go back to being a Nomad, but my fucking leg can't handle the amount of riding it takes."

"Your leg?" He stares at me, confused. "But I thought it was fine?"

I shake my head. "No. The doc told me to stop riding forever when it happened, but I refused. I did what I could to make it stronger. Well, at least strong enough so I could ride with you guys locally."

"Fuck, why didn't you tell me any of this before? I've sent you on so many runs. I never would've had I known."

"And that's why. I didn't want you to see me any differently. Hell, besides that, I know you would've blamed yourself, and I couldn't have that on my conscience. You finally found Princess and your calling being the Prez. I wasn't about to piss all over it."

He holds his hand out and I place mine in his, as his other palm comes down on my uninjured shoulder. "You're my brother, Night. Anything you need...any fuckin' thing...it's yours. You just let me know, man."

"Appreciate it."

"And you won't ever hear a word out of me about it again."

"Thank you." I don't mention those words often, but what he's saying, means a lot to me.

"Now, let's get on with church. I'm sure everyone's wondering what the hell's going on. We need to bring them all up to speed."

CHAPTER 20

Everything has changed and yet,

I am more me than I've ever been.

-Iain Thomas

BETHANY

"What do you think's happening in there?"

"I don't know, but that Lamborghini that just pulled into the parking lot?" She gestures out the window and I glance to where she points. Sure enough, there's a black sports car parked outside right next to mine and all the guys' motorcycles.

"Yeah?"

"It belongs to the Boss of the Russian Mafia."

"No fucking way." My eyes grow wide, waiting for her to explain.

"Yep."

"Why would the Mafia be here?"

"Well, you know London and Avery from the other club?"

"Yep."

"Their duo is really a trio. The third best friend, Emily, is married to the head of the Russian Mafia. Hence, the connection with the guys."

"Holy shit."

"Uh-huh. The brothers did some work with them awhile back, but I can't get into any details."

"That's still crazy he's here right now."

"I know. I'd guess that things are a little more serious than we'd anticipated. If Mafia and the other club is involved, it's a bigger threat than our guys are letting on."

"Who's that, then?" I point out the same window as a gray Phantom pulls in next.

"Holy fucking shit," she says, copying me from a minute ago, and I laugh. She turns to me and whispers, "That's Thaddaeus Morelli." The way she says it, makes him seem to be some magic creature.

"Okaaaay...Who is that, exactly?"

"Uh, that's Chicago m. o. b.!" She spells out mob, and it nearly makes me laugh. I don't, though, because this is serious according to her shocked gaze.

"So, is this bad, then?"

"Supposedly Cain did some work for him, but I've never seen him in person. I only know who he is because Viking showed me a picture in case I did ever see him."

"Wow, I wonder why they're all here at the same time. It kind of scares me being here with a ton more criminals than I'm used to."

"For once, B, it scares me too, because it means my man is knee deep in something."

"I take it he hasn't mentioned to you about whatever he's up to?"

"That would be a big fat no, but you better believe I'll be asking him tonight."

"I should ask Nightmare to tell me."

"You can, but don't be surprised if he doesn't say anything."

"Why would he keep it from me?"

"Because, it's club business. He may not tell you to keep you safe."

I hope that's not the case. I may go crazy if he doesn't share what's going on. Prissy has me a little wigged-out with all these people suddenly showing up.

"Come on," she calls and takes off out of the kitchen toward the main entry. I follow along, because I need to find out what's happening one way or another.

The heavy door opens with Cain coming through on a mission and Thaddaeus hot on his heels.

"Princess." Cain nods in acknowledgment. Of course he'd stop to greet her; she's the Prez's 'ol lady. "Bethany," he says to me next, and I nod, remaining quiet, stomach twirling with nerves.

The breath leaves me in the next moment as my hand's engulfed by a large, strong completely male hand. "Pet." His gaze meets mine, and I think my heart skips a beat when they do. "I'm Thaddaeus Morelli." His other hand falls on top of mine as he introduces himself. His deep voice invokes hot flashes. The man is the definition of GQ power and beauty. *Holy fuck.*

"Ummm...hi," I reply quietly, and Princess steps in to save me. I'm grateful for the interruption as I have no idea what to say to a man like that.

"Mr. Morelli, Cain...I'll take you to see Viking." She turns and leads the way, leaving no room for argument.

My hand is set free from his warmth, but Morelli's eyes linger on me for a moment longer and then he's gone.

My feet remain planted in the same spot as my nerves cool down. I'm going to go ahead and call that "The Thaddaeus Effect." Holy shit, if I wasn't so far gone for Nightmare, I'd probably follow that man around like a devoted groupie.

NIGHTMARE

Taking my place, I glance around at the brothers. Every one of them from ours and Ares' chapters is here, including Tate, the Boss off the Russkaya Mafiya, and Morelli, from the Chicago mob. It's like a goddamn convention for criminals taking place. Rarely do you see this many of us in one spot at the same time and usually there's either a big deal going down or cops involved if so.

"My woman was attacked today. This needs taken care of immediately," I growl, and everyone's stern gaze looks to me. I'm sure the majority of them have heard through the grapevine what went down, or, at least, the short and sweet version, but it needs to be brought up in front of everyone.

"Bethany, the woman I just met?" Morelli's cold stare lands on me, and I send one straight back. He shouldn't be speaking. He's a guest here. Clearly no one told him to shut up before he entered our clubhouse.

"Yep, she belongs to me."

"Noted." He nods with a smirk on his face.

The fucking *Joker*, huh. I'll wipe that look clean off his mouth if he gives me a reason to, and I'll do it fucking smiling the entire time too. Show him how bikers handle business.

"We'll find them all, brother," Ares growls, angry that pain has touched our club once again. He, of all people, knows how I feel. His ol' lady, Avery, has been targeted in the past. So has Twists ol' lady, Sadie, and Princess. It seems to be a favorite spot for our enemies to hit us—our women, our hearts. You'd think they'd steer clear, knowing that's a line you don't cross, but apparently, they're fucking idiots.

"All of 'em dead this time," Twist mutters, his fingers tapping in some random rhythm.

I've heard he plays guitar, and he's damn good, too. I find myself tapping out beats all the time as well. It must be a musician thing. I could use some music therapy right about now. Beating on some drums would help me get some of this energy out, that's for sure. Or a good fight. I'd take either.

"Why are you here, Thaddaeus?" Ares brings up the question we're all sitting around wondering as well. "Cain said you had business to discuss?"

"It can wait until after this other matter."

"No, go ahead," Ares orders.

"As you know, my uncle is in charge of Chicago; he runs everything with the Italians."

The majority of us are well aware of who he and his family is, so we nod and he continues.

"I want you to clean house for me. In return, I'll take over his territory and offer you the area you've been wanting."

"Shit," Ares mutters and takes a large gulp from his water bottle.

"Fuck." Viking sighs. "So you expect us to go in and do your dirty work and you'll give us a Chicago charter in return? How does this benefit us? We'll lose half our club cleaning out the mobsters up there."

"Right. In return you get your colors in my state."

"Who's to say you wouldn't turn on us, sell us out, and have your mob buddies come after us after we 'clean house' as you put it. As you can see, we're already dealin' with our own shit."

"I'm not a rat, and I'm loyal. I'm doing this because the man wronged me; otherwise. I'd never cross him. It's time I take back what was mine to begin with."

"Why would we encroach on mob territory like that? We run weapons, we deal. You guys already have your system up there."

"Right. I run all the shipping and such, meaning I could offer you a partnership in that aspect. Like I said, some things have come to light, and it's time he was dealt with."

"Break it down a little blunter for us Southern folk," 2 Piece interrupts.

"You run weapons for the mob like you do the Russians." His gaze flicks to Tate's and we all hold our breath briefly, waiting to see if we're about to have a mob war on our hands next.

After a tense moment, Tate shrugs. "We are eastern-southeastern. I don't see any conflict of interest with the Midwest, as long as you remain good on our deals we have in place. There are more of you now; I'd be an idiot to expect you to not work with others."

Viking rubs his temples, then nods at Morelli. "We'll discuss it and then vote. It's club business so everyone has to agree. We'll be in touch with what we decide."

"Good. I look forward to speaking with you soon." He stands, as does Ares and Viking. He shows them respect by shaking each of their hands and then Cain shows him back out. Cain being so close to Ares is the only reason Thaddaeus Morelli was allowed in here and heard out in the first place.

"Now, how about you, Tate?" Viking's gaze hits the Russian. It is his clubhouse, so while Ares is a President, he respects Viking's status in his own club. It's the same as when we were at church in their club last week.

"It started out as just a trip so Emily could visit with her friends. Then I caught wind that something was going on, so I left her with the girls at the other club to see if y'all needed my help. Well, the Mafiya's, specifically. Whatever's going down, do you have enough weapons or enough men to keep everyone safe? Especially after what Nightmare brought up in the beginning?"

2 Piece claps him on the shoulder, grateful. They're friends, along with Cain, because of their wives and have grown to do a lot of business together over the years. We've done some work for Tate's cousin, Beau, as well. That's actually why I got attacked by that damn lion. We were down in Mexico searching for a woman the Russians were hell bent on finding. We came away with nothing, but that's beside the point.

"We're good as far as members go, but we can always use more weapons. Did you bring anything with you?"

"I didn't, but one of my soldiers will be here tomorrow with a few cases. I figure what you don't use, you may want to sell?"

"Sounds good," Ares agrees instantly. "Brother?"

"Yeah, we're in," Viking confirms.

Tate stands next. "All right, I'll let you handle your business in private then. If I can help out, let me know." He shakes Viking and Ares' hands on his way out.

What a busy damn day. I swear it seems nice and quiet around here and then everything comes at the club all at once. Shit can never just trickle in to be dealt with one at a time.

"Fuck, now back to what we're going to do to catch these assholes." Vike takes another swig of his drink and continues. "Spidey, run that photo of Shadow you took today through your face program."

"Will do, Boss. I'll let you know what I find."

"I've called the other Nomads, Exterminator and Ruger. They're on their way into town to provide some backup, but let's hope we don't need any. The rest of the crew is on a run up north so they won't be heading down with them. The mess at Nightmare's crib is cleaned up. I say we go on full lock-down until we figure out what the fuck to do next. They got a little too close to home today, and I don't want to see it happen to anyone else, especially when we haven't even found their location."

"I agree. We need to vote. All in favor of the plan?" Ares finishes, and we go around the table agreeing.

With church coming to an end, the brothers and I pile out into the bar area while Spider runs the photos he got of Shadow through everything he can think of. I've barely thrown back half a beer, and, in no time, he's calling us to his room to see what all he's found.

Blaze, Viking, Ares, Cain, and I all pile in and take a look while he explains everything he was able to uncover. He found it in mere minutes with the right information to search for. Fucking crazy how you can be hunted down through random cameras positioned throughout the world.

"So, the facial recognition was able to pick up Shadow all over the place. One in particular was his mugshot which came paired with his legal name. It also found him at several gas stations that have been under surveillance after being robbed. Lucky for us, he had several buddies with him during these times. I was able to feed those camera shots into the system and figure out where a cluster of them have been gathering."

"A cluster?" Blaze's eyes row wide, glancing at Viking.

"Yep, not a small one, either. It looks like they've been holed up in a little town four hours north of here. My guess is they did it on purpose, waiting to make their move. It's way too damn convenient they're that close and they weren't planning something."

Ares grumbles, "I don't get it. How could everyone miss them? We have allies everywhere. It doesn't add up, none of it."

"Actually, it does. The spot where they're hiding out is technically Oklahoma, which puts them out of our main territory. And it's also right off a busy highway so they can be on and off in no time, with hardly anyone seeing them. In this case, random gas stations were the only thing that pulled them up. If Shadow hadn't got caught by Nightmare, there's a chance we never would've caught on. They're smart, and I hate admitting that about enemies."

"Makes sense." Cain shrugs. "Random Casinos run by the Indians, pussy, drugs, all right there, and not closely monitored 'cause it's Indian Territory."

Viking huffs, cursing. "Where are the fucking Indian bikers in all this? We couldn't go through Oklahoma on a run without them being up our asses for a payout to pass through."

Blaze tsks. "I'm sure they're getting a payout somehow. You know the Iron Fists roll around in heroin and meth. Bet they're cooking some shit up for the Indians to keep quiet. The entire thing smells bad to me."

"Goddamn, motherfucker," Ares mumbles, rubbing his temples. "The fuck we gonna do then? We can't go guns blazin' on the goddamn Indian reservation; Uncle Sam would be breathing down our throats in a heartbeat. We've gotten around with mild heat for many years, not trying to get in trouble with them now."

"Actually," Spider interrupts. Smart little fucker has an answer for everything. "Where they are, it's not technically the reservation. It's closer to the Texas line, so if I give you a location you should be fine. You have to light it up and get the fuck outta there though. No sticking around to see the outcome. It would be hit it and quit it."

"Good work, Spidey." Viking claps his shoulder. "Get us a location, and we'll plan a visit."

"We need to discuss this ASAP," I mutter as we pile into the hallway.

"We'll have a drink and wait for Spider to finish. When he's done, we'll go back into church. I think everyone's still here." Viking glances at us and Ares nods.

"Sounds good, brother. It's been a while since I've had some fun. I'm ready to take care of business."

"Brothers, we have news," Viking begins as we're all crammed back into church, Spider with printouts spread on the table in front of him. "We have a location and an estimate in numbers."

"'Bout time, let's finish this," Twist grits, and I couldn't agree with him more.

"Ares and I discussed a plan we'd like to run over with everyone. We're wanting to pay them another visit like before. Think Cali all over again. We torch the place and get the fuck out of there. Come home and batten down for potential blowback. We can knock a bunch of them out with one big hit. Let them scamper away like roaches, same as they did the last time."

"We all going?" Torch questions, ready to get down and dirty. He used to be a Widow Maker in South Carolina before they were patched over, along with Blaze and Bronx. He's a pretty mean fucker; I have respect for him always keeping his word.

"We'll have Exterminator and Ruger; I know they'll want to be in. From our charter: Chaos, Torch, Nightmare, and I will go." His irises flick to mine. "If you're up for it?" Everyone else's gaze falls on me as well. He's never asked before, but I know he wants to make sure I can handle the ride with my leg. I'm touched and irritated all in the same breath.

"Of course," I mutter, glowering so I don't come off as a weak spot in front of anyone.

"Scot, Bronx, Blaze, and Spidey will stay here to hold down the club."

"I'm going, too," Twist interrupts and Ares growls.

"Yeah, Twist, Cain, Snake, and I will ride up. The rest of my charter will stay at the club."

"Everyone good with it?"

"Aye," we each respond pegging our gaze on Viking and Ares.

Enough fucking around. I'm ready to leave right the fuck now and handle this shit. I'm sure the others are antsy as well.

"Everyone watch your backs until then. We'll see what Tate's men bring up and then plan to hit the road the following day. Expect to ride out Friday. Those assclowns will get fucked up Friday, and we'll be able to surprise their asses when they least expect it." Ares and Viking rise, done with business for the time being.

The only thing on my mind is finding Bethany and kissing her again. Her lips were perfect earlier.

Sapphire Knight

CHAPTER 21

His love roared louder

than her demons.

- |writtenbyhim.

BETHANY

I'm half asleep by the time Nightmare crawls into bed behind me. Maverick's passed out right next to me on a cot Princess found in the storage room. It's a tight fit in here, but we'll make-do for a few days. It's not so bad either, since I've gotten used to sleeping next to Night most of the time, and we have to share a bed here.

"Mmm, you smell so fuckin' good," he whispers in my ear, and I can make out whiskey laced with mint on his breath. He must've been drinking with his brothers a bit before and then swished with mouthwash before coming to bed.

"And you smell like whiskey and mouthwash." I grin and he chuckles.

"Sounds like a damn good combination to me." He wraps his strong arm around my waist, pulling me into his warmth. It's like being covered with a fluffy blanket, and I love the feeling.

"It is."

"You finally gonna let me in your pants, baby?"

"And there's the whiskey talking."

"Dollface..." It's nearly a whine which makes me laugh.

"Oh no, you don't crawl in bed half-lit and expect me to spread 'em for you, the first time in years, at that. Maybe eventually, but not tonight, handsome."

"You think I'm handsome?" he asks in an unsure mumble.

"Of course, you're handsome. You're freaking hot. I'm not afraid to admit that much. Besides, you know it anyhow, all those chicks going crazy over you when you play the drums."

"That's just the rocker vibe. But *you* think that, even with the scar and fucked up colored eye?"

Can he really be unsure about it? I would never peg him being insecure about anything, or caring for that matter. He's nuts if he doesn't realize women love mismatched eyes and scars like that. He's not only gorgeous, but he's got the bad-boy-kind-of-scary-but-damn-I-could-fuck-you kind of look going—always.

"I think your eyes are beautiful, and the scar is sexy."

"Hmm...You're beautiful."

"And you're horny."

"I am," he admits and I grind my ass against him just to tease him a bit.

"You're bad, Bethany, and bad one's get spanked. You better watch it or I'll pull those panties down, then you'll be begging to be fucked."

"Jesus Christ, why do you have to say shit like that? Our son is right next to us. I can't go at it; you know I could never be quiet when you were in full-on pound town mode."

He chuckles, and it sends tingles all over me. He sounds absolutely delicious. "Fine, but I'm having some fun," he declares as the palm resting on my stomach flattens and skims under the elastic of my panties.

"Ummm...whoa, buddy," I sputter as his palm rests over my clit and he applies some pressure.

"Enough being patient," he grumbles, his soft lips coming to my neck where he nips and sucks the tender area.

Holding my breath so I don't squirm and intensify the erotic tingles, I go with it, closing my eyes in the moment. It takes everything in me not to be loud with him. I don't know what it is, why he gets me so flustered like he does, but it's like his hands are magic.

I have to be quiet, but it doesn't mean I can't enjoy his touch, the feeling of him holding me so closely to him. I've wanted Nightmare since the first day I set my eyes on him. He's absolutely crazy if he doesn't realize how gorgeous he is or how women gawk when they see him. Fucking sinful is more accurate.

His middle finger dips between my folds making me gasp. It's been too long since I've felt him. Everything is right on the edge, wanting to explode and waiting for his next move.

He leans over a bit and I turn my face to him, letting him take my mouth with his. As his tongue strokes mine, his finger sinks into my depth. He catches the moan that attempts to escape from my lips, keeping all of me for himself.

Pulling my bottom lip between his, he bites it, just rough enough to make my eyes pop back open. He's wearing a wicked smile. The fucker knows he turns me to putty with his touch.

"Feel good, dollface?"

"Yes, fantastic."

"Oh yeah, that good, huh? How about when I do this?" He dips another finger in, moving them in long strokes. His thumb circles my clit at the same time, and it's a miracle I can breathe or think through the sensations.

"Fucking shit," leaves me on a breathy gasp. So unladylike but I could care less. He knows exactly what it means.

"Yeah?" he growls, his teeth biting at my bottom lip again. My eyes roll back, submitting to his blissful torture. Smelling him, feeling him, hearing him—all have my body waving the white flag to whatever he wants to do with it.

His fingers plunging in deep has my mouth popping open. He uses the opportunity to kiss me again. It's the feelings that the best types of dreams are made of. The twists and flutters spiraling all around as you're enraptured in the sweetest bit of euphoria between a man and a woman.

"I want you seeing motherfuckin' stars when you look at me, baby," he admits. If he only knew. He's been making me see stars for far too long already.

"I do, oh God, I do."

"Fireworks, Bethany."

His growl has me wanting to climb over him and ride him like a fucking cowgirl. I'm not one, never have been, but pretty sure I could give him one hell of a ride to convince him differently.

"I do."

"Swear to me."

"I swear." I'll tell him anything he wants to hear. The only thing clouding my mind is the building orgasm and the fact that it's Nightmare giving it to me.

"It's what I saw when you had my cock in your mouth—stars. Fucking bright-ass stars and your beautiful face. Had me shooting my load off like no other." His finger presses against my nub harder, and the breath catches in my throat.

"Now, dollface, give me more fucking stars," he orders, pressing his fingers in me, stroking quicker, and I explode.

My pussy quivers with delight, attempting to pull him in deeper as my body rides the wave of pleasure. The wave that only Nightmare makes me feel whenever

I'm with him—no one else. No other man can play my body so easily and make it do whatever he wants it to; they never even come close.

"Night." Groaning, my hand clutches his forearm to me, not letting him move away immediately. The aftershocks flutter through, and he waits patiently while dropping kisses all along my neck. I could lie here and let him pepper kisses all night long and be a happy woman.

"I saw stars."

"Promise?" he whispers against my throat.

I nod and the only dreams that come that night are ones filled with a broody man, there to protect and love me. They're the best types of dreams to have.

NIGHTMARE

"You have to leave?" Bethany peers up at me, worried.

"I do."

"Please be careful."

"I will."

I stuff the saddlebags with my belongings. She stands at the back of my bike, holding Maverick's hand as they watch me. Everyone's loading up, a few of us having to say good-bye to our other halves. We haven't made anything official or said it out loud, but that's what she is to me. Maverick is just icing on the cake when it comes to our family. I'd do anything for that kid.

"I feel like we've barely had time to reconnect," she admits, biting her bottom lip.

Nodding, I stand and pull her into my arms, Maverick's hand wrapping around my thigh. "It'll be all right. Once I get back, we'll have more time," I mumble in her hair.

"Princess told me what happened with this group before; just watch your back. You have a kid waiting for you."

"Just a kid?" I pull her in my arms, holding her tighter.

"You have me, too."

I nod again, taking in the flowery scent from her shampoo. "Go inside. I probably won't call you or text 'cause I'll be riding most the time."

"If you aren't coming back right away for some reason, you need to at least text."

"I will, I promise." Pulling back, I press my lips to hers gently. I want to own her mouth, kiss her roughly to take as much as possible, but I don't. I'm gentle, giving her my sweet side, relishing in her taste so I can easily remember it later.

"Later alligator." Putting my fist out, Mav bumps it with his, giving me a happy grin.

"Bye, Daddy."

In no time we're loaded up, our engines shaking the ground as the nine of us take off on a mission of revenge. It's time to head to Oklahoma and fuck some shit up.

CHAPTER 22

**There is my heart, and then
there is you, and I'm not sure
there is a difference.
-A.R. Asher**

"What is it?" Viking growls as we pull off at a gas station out of turn. We'd already filled up and were set for another two hours at least before breaking.

"Fuck, I don't know, but my phone has been going off nonstop, continuous for the past hour."

"Just Bluetooth that shit, we're wasting too much time."

"I would, but I can't hear good with that thing in my ear. Besides, who the fuck you know would be callin' me like that? Someone who's lost their motherfuckin' mind," I grit in return, and pull my device out to see what the hell is going on.

It says **Bethany: 240 missed calls**.

"What the ever loving fuck?" Holding it up to Vike, his gaze widens, and he gestures for me to call. I was going too anyhow.

"The fuck's goin' on, Bethany, Christ?" I damn near yell when she answers.

She's sobbing, and I can't understand a damn thing she's saying. "Baby, calm your tits, the fuck happen?"

She's crying something fierce, mumbling words that make no sense whatsoever. She's hysterical to the point I would be thinking of sedating her if I were there, and it's crushing me inside. "I cannot understand you at all. Is Princess there? Put her on so she can talk."

"Nightmare?" Princess comes on the line; no doubt she's been crying, too. I hear Viking swear in the background, once he powers his cell on and discovers his missed calls too. Her voice has me on edge; this is the Ice Queen I'm talking to. She doesn't show weakness like this, especially to me or to anyone besides her ol' man.

"Yeah, the fuck's goin' on over there?"

"Y-you guys need to come back, right now."

"Why? Talk to me, damn it!" I shout, and all the guys stare at me, with 'what the fuck' expressions.

"They have him. They took Maverick. You guys left and so many showed up. They killed Bronx; ripped a knife up his stomach and pulled his guts out in the middle of the parking lot. Scot...he's gone. Th-they cut his fucking throat! Blaze is barely breathing; I have the doc coming right now." She lets out a shuddering breath, her voice choking up as she fights to get words out. "But Mav, h-h-h-he-he's gone, Nightmare. We fought them; I swear to God, we fought. But there were just too many. They threw us to the side like flies. Puppet, their leader said they were leaving me and Bethany alive to warn you. They s-said the Fists always collect their debts owed."

I growl into the line, my mind beginning to spiral out of control with the many ways I'll kill them all, and she continues.

"We took a son from them, so they're taking a son from us. Oh God, Night, I don't know what to do. Bethany is losing it; she's going to kill herself at this rate. You guys have to get here now. There's blood everywhere, and her son's gone. I-I don't know what to do."

"Keep her safe. Call 2 Piece and tell him to get over there now."

"I've been calling everyone; I think the Fists are hitting them too. It didn't seem like they were finished when they left."

"Call your father. Tie B up if you have to; I don't give a fuck. Just watch her. We will be there as quickly as possible," I order calmly, even though I feel nothing of the sort. Every nerve in my skin is jumping, and I'm so angry I could peel someone's skin off their body with my bare hands and feed it into a fire piece by bloody piece at this moment.

I hang up, stuffing the phone in my pocket. Everyone stares at me in anticipation. I'm so fucked up inside, yet I have to tell them what has happened. I have to find the strength.

Climbing off my bike, I stumble a few steps away and then puke. I wretch up every last thing in my stomach, eventually dry heaving, with the strong taste of stomach acid left behind in my throat. It takes an empty stomach before I'm able to pull it together enough to speak.

I turn to my brothers with tears in my eyes. Swallowing, I take in each of their faces and then relay everything Princess just told me on the phone.

Viking is on his bike and out of the parking lot before I even finish. We all follow quickly, and it's amazing I can even concentrate enough to ride. All I know is that my son is gone, my girl is an absolute wreck, and I have to get the fuck back home.

I have to fix this; I will fix this, if not for me and my club, for Bethany.

The ride home is the longest I've ever been on. I shook the entire way, not just my hands, but the inside of my stomach quaked with worry and anger. I have no idea what to even do. Should I just hold Bethany while she cries, or should I immediately hunt down the bastards that have my son?

I decide on both. As soon as I see her, I wrap my arms around her battered body and just breathe as she sobs into my chest. Tears fall down my cheeks hearing her so beyond broken. How do you get through something like this? What on earth do you say to someone who just had her child literally ripped from her hands, in a place where she should've been safe?

They came into our home, killed members, and stole our son. There's nothing I can say to bring her peace in this moment. I'm barely standing upright on my own two feet.

I can't remember the last time I shed even a tear for anything at all, but my cheeks are wet as her body shakes against mine. I have to be strong for her, for him, but I feel anything but. My physical being feels weak and beat down all over, I'm not even the one who took any of the physical blows either.

Two brothers are dead and gone forever. If anyone could've been somewhat of a father figure to me, it would've been Scot. The man never passed any judgment and welcomed me immediately when he recognized I was young and lost. He led us for a time with the Nomads, and I'm honored to have had the chance to ride with him for so many years.

Bronx was just a fuckin' kid. I'd only known him since he patched over from the Widow Makers. He'd barely cleared his Prospect patch and been patched a full member with us. He was a punk the first time I'd come across him, and I'd gotten the pleasure to watch him evolve into a young man. He'd grown into someone honest and loyal over the past few years, someone worthy of wearing the Oath Keeper patch.

I can't help but have the festering rage building inside me toward Twist. I know I shouldn't blame a brother for what has happened, but his woman brought the Iron Fists to their front door initially. They'd had run ins and issues with the club trying to claim our territory, but it was her that brought the brunt. It's because of them that my son isn't here with his family right now.

We never should've ridden off and torched that clubhouse for them in Cali. The Nomads should've told them to take care of their own shit. But we were the hard ones, the true death dealers of the club. When shit hit the fan, they called us, and we were there to answer. Now it's us who needs the help, my woman and me. Every motherfucker better step up to help out, too.

Saying a silent prayer to a God I'd long stopped believing in, I can only hope I was wrong. Hope that He's up there, listening to my heartfelt plea for assistance and helps me find my son and some peace in this life. Why is it we have to hit a new level of low to seek comfort and redemption from up above? It took a three year old to bring me to my knees and want to change my ways. I want to become a better man in life not for me, but for him and for Bethany.

She shutters and I keep holding her, trying to give her some ounce of warmth to keep her with me. Bethany's so fucked up, I'm afraid she's mentally checked the fuck out. She weeps and stares into space. She won't speak to me. She mumbles his name and sobs some more. She's broken, and I can't fix her, but I'm hoping to get our son back because I know he can fix her.

Daydream

"I have you baby. I will do everything to make this better, I promise you with everything I am. I'm so fuckin' sorry. I will get our son back if it's the last thing I ever do," I murmur in her hair, my voice laced with heartbreak, rocking her in my grip.

She doesn't answer, just cries more and I feel like each tear that falls from her eyes rips more of my soul from my chest. I'll be completely black inside by the time this is over. My heart will match the bruises on her face.

"I have Spider searching any cameras in the area. We'll find them," Viking declares, but part of me doesn't want to hear him. A piece of me is locking up and pulling away from everyone. If I don't get Maverick back, I know I will never be able to forgive my brothers or this club. Whether it's their fault this has happened or not, I will hold them responsible for my pain.

One thing is for certain: I will never stop looking for him.

"I'm so sorry, Daydream," I repeat, not able to convey my true feelings. I wish I knew how, but I don't. All I know is the person I love is hurt, sad, and broken, and the other person I love is missing.

The doc finds us after fixing up Princess to check over B. Once she completes her exam, she asks if I want a sedative. I don't take one, but have her inject Bethany with a mild tranquilizer.

She's too fucked up right now. She may hurt herself, and I can't let that happen. I'm here and I have to protect her, even if that's from herself.

She'll probably end up hating me for all of this, and I can't blame her for that. One thing I've come to discover, though, is that I love her a great deal more than I'd begun to realize these past weeks. She's it for me—the one—my everything, and that includes Maverick. So she can hate me. I'll take it, own it, and wear that badge every day of my life. But, I'm going to do whatever I have to, to make her love me like I do her, with every single beat of my cold, once-dead heart.

CHAPTER 23

I love how you take care of
me. How you keep working to be
a better man. Even on days I fail
to be a better woman.
-IntentionalToday.com

BETHANY

The days come and go, passing me in what feels
like a drug-induced haze. I let Nightmare be my
strength.

I've been strong for the past few years. I took care of Mav when he was sick, up all night crying through fevers and puking. I took him to the hospital when he stepped on that rusty nail and held his hand and promised him the entire world to get him through his pain. I've been brave for him each time he's gotten scared, but this time I just can't do it. I need someone to be strong and brave for me, and that's Nightmare.

He takes it in stride, letting me cry when I feel that I need to. He accepts my hits each time I blame him, and he stands still when I pound on his chest in anger. Most of all, through everything, he keeps trying and he shows me love.

He loves me so much, that if my little boy wasn't missing, my heart would be so full, it would overflow. Through the anger consuming me over my son being taken by a rival club, I love Nightmare in return. I hold on to him for dear life and let him take the reins, knowing inside that he won't let me drown. He can't, because I won't survive on my own anymore.

NIGHTMARE

My cell rings, and it's a number I've never seen before. "Yeah?" I answer, not in the mood to deal with spam calls. I may rip their throats out if presented with the opportunity.

"This Nightmare?" A gravelly voice replies.

"Yep, who the fuck is this?"

"I'm the one keeping your son alive."

"Motherfucker! You better not hurt him, or I'll—"

"You'll do what?" he interrupts, chuckling. "You forget, I'm the one in control."

"Fine." My voice is dark, coated in fury, wanting to rip him to shreds as I do my best not to plead. "What the fuck do you want so I can have my kid back?"

"Oh, I'm afraid that's not going to happen. It's quite simple, you see. You took something from me, now I take it back."

"What did I ever take from you?"

"Well for starters, your other club took my son."

"I'm not responsible for that!"

"I know that, but you took something from me as well."

"I don't even know who the fuck you are!" I can't stop the shouting. I'm so pissed, I feel like my head is going to explode.

"Shadow was my son, and you killed him."

"He was at my house, threatening my woman."

"He wouldn't have hurt her. He was only there for the child. Like I told the women, you take a son from me, I'll take one from you."

"Why? Why my son? There are so many other members that have club brats."

"I know that, we've been watching. However, *your* charter was the one to torch my clubhouse in Cali. So when that sexy bitch Bethany showed up with your kid in tow, it was the perfect opportunity to get my payback."

"So you've been watching the entire time and planning to take him since she showed up?"

"I have...and now he's mine."

"The fuck he is. I will find you, and I will get my son back."

"No, you won't, but I have a deal for you. You'll get him back, eventually. He's going to be raised by me, and when he's a grown man, I'll let him go back to you. If he wishes."

"Not fucking happening," I grit and the line goes dead, making me shout.

Throwing my phone against the wall, it smashes and I begin to hyperventilate. His words crawled right under my skin and have begun to fester already. I think he's crazy enough to believe what he's doing is in his right. He can't take my son and keep him.

That's medieval shit, sending your kid to live off with the enemy or another king. In our case a rival club and I'm assuming Puppet is the President over them all. We didn't snuff out the Iron Fists; we poked the fucking nest and now they've come back to swarm.

I'd heard they were a hard club—hell, we all had. That was why we were sent in the first place. We were warned that they don't fuck around. Neither did we. At least I thought we didn't. Clearly we had no fucking clue what the hell we were doing.

There's so much more here, so much under the surface. I can't just kill the Fists I find like I'd want to; this is going to take planning. How the fuck can I possibly pull this off? There has to be a way.

To think the Iron Fists have just been sitting back and waiting, biding their time for retaliation. We were stupid enough to believe we'd outdone them. The opportunity arose, and they took it, leading us straight into a goddamn trap. I'd bet their clubhouse isn't even in Oklahoma. It was all a ruse to make the club weak enough for them to easily take what they intended.

"Talk to me," Ex grumbles.

They haven't left yet; he and Ruger have been by my side waiting to help me—everyone has. We buried Scot and Bronx yesterday, but I wasn't present. I loved my brothers, but I have my own shit to deal with. I know if they were here they would understand and want me to keep looking for Maverick.

"What's going on?" Viking asks immediately, noticing me flipping my shit. I puke again. I've lost weight this week from being sick so much, but it's the only way my body is coping with the stress and pressure I'm under.

"Breathe, brother; tell us what just happened." Chaos rests his hand on my shoulder, another good friend of mine, having my back. Regardless, without Mav I will blame them, no matter how much I tell myself not to.

"It was him," I get out between heaves.

I feel like my chest is seizing up, and I'm having a fucking panic attack or some shit. I can't breathe. It feels like my ribs are squeezing me in a vice grip. Like my heart's going to burst straight through my chest. It's not like running too much. It's like sticking your head under water and being forced to suck in nothing but water. It fills your lungs, weighing your body down, choking you the fuck out.

My vision goes blurry for a moment, and I puke again, but this time nothing comes out. I have nothing left to expel. Acidic aftermath fills my mouth and I gag a few times. The blurred vision is new and not something I want sticking around.

Eventually it passes and I'm able to explain what just happened. I tell them about Puppet and everything that was said. I feel like I'm losing my mind, like this is all a sick joke or a goddamn nightmare and I need to wake up.

Letting it hit me all over, I shut down and go on a rampage, punching and throwing everything I can find. I down a bottle of Jager and then upchuck it all back up, damn near immediately. It gets so bad that I'm pricked with something in my back, and then everything goes black.

BETHANY

Princess shakes me awake, upset.

"What's happening?" It leaves me in a groggy mumble as I meet her concerned gaze.

"It's time for you to snap out of it, B."

"I can't deal with this, Prissy. There's nothing I can do." Brushing her off, I fall back against the pillows. My body aches from lying around and sleeping so much. I have to, though; I can't handle being awake and not being able to do anything. No one here will let me leave to go find my son. No one has answers. I can't cope like this.

"The fuck you can't," she replies angrily and suddenly she's straddling my waist. She rears back and unleashes a harsh slap. Copper overtakes my mouth as my lip splits on the inside, and, for the first time in a week, I'm seeing her face clearly. "Shit is happening!" she screams, her bruised face scrunching up in sadness and anger. "No more, Bethany. You've fucking slept and moped for a week."

"Well excuse the fuck out of me, Mrs. Fucking Perfect, but my son was stolen from your husband's club!" I shout back and the bitch rears back, hitting me again.

It's enough to infuriate me to the point of throwing her off my waist and jumping out of bed. "Bitch!" I yell, my hand coming to my face as I get some distance from her.

"Do I have your attention now?"

"Yes. What. The. Fuck."

"Time to pull yourself together and stop being selfish. Your man lost his shit today, and he needs you. He's doing what he can to hold it together for the both of you, but girlfriend he's fucking falling. He got a call last night about Maverick that rocked him. He went off the deep end, and your ass needs to pull him the fuck back so he can get your son!"

"What do you mean? What call? Tell me what the fuck you're talking about, Princess."

"Nice to finally have your damn attention. We need coffee and I'll explain everything to you."

Hours pass as he sleeps, and I pace the clubhouse like a caged animal. Princess was right. I needed coffee, and then I needed her to hold me while I broke again after hearing what Puppet told Night. And then I became angry. It's what's keeping me going right now waiting for Nightmare to wake up. He freaked his brothers out so badly, they fed him a mild horse tranquilizer. Thank God the man's the size of a mountain or they could've killed him.

"Ermmm," he mumbles, waking from his own fog. He's been asleep since last night.

"I should fucking punch you for letting them knock you out. Really, Nightmare, a whole bottle of Jager?"

"Huh?" His sleepy gaze meets mine, bloodshot to hell. "You're up?"

"Well one of us had to be since they put you out."

"They put me out?"

"Yes, sleeping beauty. Now wake the fuck up and find our son, it's been long enough."

"What happened to your face?"

"The new shit? Princess."

"Jesus, I don't even want to know."

"It was my wake-up call, now here is yours. Get up, get your shit together or I'll be the one stabbing you in the throat." I hold my hand out, coffee cup near the brim. He's going to need it just like I did.

"I can't believe you're out here." He sits up from one of the couches in the bar.

"In the flesh." I hand him the coffee and take a seat beside him. "We need a plan, Night. This self-destruction shit we're doing to ourselves is getting us nowhere. We'll be stronger together and our son needs us to save him. No one else will."

"All right then, what did you have in mind?"

CHAPTER 24

You put your arms around

me and I'm home.

-Love Quotes

"You think your plan will work?" Prissy asks, sitting across from me in the kitchen.

I haven't eaten in days, and I'm trying to choke down some soup to get some strength back. We're failing Maverick, and he doesn't deserve this. He needs to have two parents he can count on who will go into battle for him. We have to fight for him; I'll never forgive myself if we don't.

I can only imagine how scared he must be, away from everyone and everything he knows. And I have no idea if Puppet is being nice to him or even feeding him. I have to have faith with what we know.

Puppet said that he wanted to keep Maverick until he was grown, so I have to think that he's feeding him. I need to keep telling myself that he's okay so I don't lose it again and go off the deep end.

"It has too. We don't have any options, and I refuse to let this shitbag keep my kid. I don't care if Nightmare killed his son or not. Shadow was a grown-ass man and knew what he was doing. Maverick is a three year old little boy; he has no part in any of this. I can't believe we missed his birthday. That piece of shit not only stole Mav from me, but his third birthday. The first one Nightmare was going to get to celebrate, too, and it was stolen away."

"I know it, B; I wish we could freaking gut Puppet for this. I don't normally want such evil to touch someone, but I hope this guy slowly rots for what he's done. If the brothers have any say in how Puppet goes, we can have faith that they'll make it very painful."

"I want to do it myself, Prissy. I told Nightmare that they need to catch him alive because I want to be the one to end him. He says we have to wait, though, and that as much as he wants him gone, the Fists are more than what they originally thought. Nightmare believes our revenge will take time to get."

She remains quiet, picking at her sandwich. I've never had hate for someone like I do for Puppet. I want to take his life like he so easily has taken mine.

Daydream

That evening we crawl into bed; this time, together. It's the first time since Maverick has been missing. After seeing Night so messed up over everything, I know he needs me. I have to show him that he's loved and that I believe in him. Without him on his game, none of this will work the way we need it to.

"I spoke to Spider; he's going to hack into the phone company to get me the number that called before I broke my phone."

"So we'll get to call tomorrow then?"

"Yeah. Spider said he'll have it for us first thing along with a new untraceable phone."

"Good. I really hope this works."

"It will. Puppet was livid over losing his own flesh. He'll be all over this new information."

I nod, trying to stay positive. This will work. It has to. If not, I have no idea what to do.

Night kisses my shoulder softly and I pull him to me, feathering kisses all over his face. It's like worry lines have appeared out of nowhere. My beautiful man is falling apart. I don't know if it's because he's exhausting his body or if the stress of it all is making them suddenly appear deeper. I hate seeing him like this; he's normally so strong.

My kiss lands on his lips next and he takes it up a notch, adding his skillful tongue to the mix. Within seconds his hand's under my shirt, squeezing my breasts and tweaking my nipples. It feels divine to have my mind distracted for the first time in what feels like forever. I'm mentally drained, and his touch is a blissful reprieve.

"I want you," I whisper, my nails dig into his forearm, begging for more.

"Yeah?" His husky breath trails over my shoulder as he presses more kisses to a spot I never realized could be so erotic. "I always want you, Daydream," he states as his hand pushes my yoga pants down, freeing my lower half to him to do with as he pleases.

His warm palm disappears momentarily to push his boxer briefs down and then he's pushing his length inside me from behind. His cock stretches my center, the burn a welcome feeling.

"Ah," groaning lowly as he sinks in deeper.

"You okay?"

"Mmmhmm."

One more push as he grips my hip tightly with his fingers and he's seated in me fully. It's been years since I've felt him down there, and it was never like this. It was never soft and gentle like he's showing me right now.

His lips work their way to my back, kissing and biting me sweetly, enough to cause my hips to jump eagerly.

"I missed you." It takes a lot inside for me to admit feelings I've kept locked away, hidden from the world. But my words are true; I did miss him. Everything about him, especially the way he feels when he fills me so fully.

At my admission, his teeth sink into my shoulder as he thrusts just a touch rougher.

"Keep saying shit like that dollface. I love hearing you talk."

"Even here, like this?'

"Especially like this. You mean everything to me, B. Wish you'd see that."

My throat grows tight and I swallow through the impending tears wanting to appear. Now's not the time for them, but he just said something I've wanted to hear leave his mouth for years. Growing up, I didn't think there was a man out there for me; I'm too much of a mess. Turns out I needed someone just as messy to get me and need me, to love me and keep me, like I want them to.

"I hope so, Night, 'cause I don't know if I can continue to go through life without you."

"You don't have to, I'm here," he rasps as his mouth makes a blissful assault to my neck. His thrusts grow rhythmic, playing my body in its own sweet melody he's slowly creating.

He needs me to show him love right now, but I didn't realize that I needed him to show me love too. When you're a mom you learn to put your desires on hold. But Nightmare's breaking through that, slowly filling up holes I didn't know existed. He's making me complete, and the crazy thing is, it's all happening in the opposite order.

Usually relationships begin, and you get time to build on to them, to be happy and in love before you face obstacles. For us, it's been completely different. One thing after another we've been fighting through. At first, we fought against each other. Now, we fight against them together and it's an entirely new feeling to have.

"Don't leave me again," he mutters in my ear, pushing inside deep.

"I won't." I reach back, my hand weaving into his hair, keeping his mouth to me.

"Promise me, baby."

"I promise, Night, I promise." Moaning, my legs clamp together tighter, making him feel even bigger as he glides in from behind.

"I want stars, Bethany," he orders, and I nod, concentrating on the amazing feeling, letting my orgasm build. He's so damn bossy, but I love it.

"Please." The moan leaves me on a breath, but I have no idea what I'm asking for.

He does though, as his grip on my hip tightens and his drive increases. He pumps into me over and over, pushing me over the edge. "Stars," I gasp and he growls, finding his own release as I spiral through mine as well.

"You fuckin' blow me away, B." He pulls free after a moment, moving to lie on his back.

"That's not the only thing I blow." I turn to him winking, and for the first time this week, he grins.

Day made.

NIGHTMARE

Spider hands me the new phone with the number already programmed in. I'm shaky. I want to call, but then I don't. The last conversation I had with this motherfucker made me lose my shit. I don't want B seeing me like that or my brothers for that matter.

My gaze meets hers. She looks hopeful, and it gives me some strength. Taking a deep breath, I hit dial.

"What the fuck do you want?" is said when he answers.

Obviously, this crooked dick already knows who the hell's calling. Bethany told me they'd stolen her phone before they took off. Spider tried searching for it, but they must've just used it to get my number and then turned it back off.

"You know what I want, motherfucker."

"Ain't happenin', cunt, done told ya' that."

"That was before. But you don't know what I know."

"Cute, doubt it'll help ya sort it out."

"You'd be surprised."

"Hurry up then."

"You said a son for a son, but what if I told you that you had a grandson? A grandson with your own blood running through his veins?"

"Oh, you're good. Stop trying to fuck with me."

"Swear to God, this kid was Ghost's."

"Ghost?" His voice comes out a bit unsure all of a sudden.

"Yep, and I happen to know who was pregnant with his baby when he was killed."

"If you're lying, you'll never see your son again. This, I promise you."

"It's no lie. I want my kid back, and I'll throw any motherfucker under the bus to achieve my goal."

"Noted. You expect me to give little Maverick up just for some information? If so, you're mistaken."

"What if I could arrange for you to meet this kid? He looks just like your piece-of-shit son. He's close to my son's age, so plenty of time to become a part of his life."

"A part of his life? Ha, if what you say is true, that kid should be here. He'd be treated like the club prince he is."

"Well, you'd have to go through my brother, Twist. He killed your son and is raising your grandson as his own kid. He'd drill you full of holes before he let you anywhere near him. But, I could arrange it."

"And, in return, you want your kid back?"

"I wouldn't help you otherwise."

"Who says I need your fucking help? You couldn't keep your own kid safe."

"Listen fuck face, I didn't know he was in any sort of danger or you would've never been able to breathe the same fuckin' air as him. You want to meet your grandson, you go through me, and I get my kid back. That's the only way this works. Your grandson is so well hidden, you'd never get to him."

Daydream

"Fine. But I don't give Maverick up until I get a DNA confirmation. If he's really my blood, then send me a lock of his hair, and it will match with mine. If not, your son is toast after this scheme."

At his words, I choke out, "Done." I want to retch, thinking of him harming Mav.

"Have it tomorrow. Go to the market and give it to a cashier named Sonya. I'll call you when I get the results."

"Let me talk to my son."

"Fine." He speaks to a few people, and then my heart shatters in a million pieces as the small voice comes over the line.

"Ummm...Daddy?"

"Mav!" I shout. "Shit, are you okay? We love you, Mav, we'll get you home. I promise you, son." I ramble until Puppet's demented laughter comes over the line.

"I'll be in touch." He hangs up.

Handing the phone to Bethany, I turn away from her. She has tears coating her cheeks, and it's more than I can take. I puke up my toast from earlier in the nearest trash can. My body won't stop shaking either; it's to the point where it looks like that shaking disease folks get sometimes.

Dainty arms wrap around me from behind, her face pressed into my back, just holding me. She's giving me her strength and I need every bit I can get. I couldn't let her be the one to speak to Puppet, to allow him to taunt her like that.

"It's okay, Nightmare. He bought it, and that was the first step."

287

"Twist will never forgive me. I'm trading one son for another," I reply, shaking my head, sick with myself.

"No, we're doing what we have to, to get our son back. They brought this on us, we never asked for this. Now we do what we have to in order to protect Maverick, even if that means giving up a club secret."

"You realize my brothers can kill me for this?" I turn, finally facing her so she can see the sorrow in my eyes. I may get Maverick back, but there's a good chance I'll be taken from both of them.

"Listen to me, if that happens, we'll run."

"No, we won't. I ran one time in my life when my father was killed. Never again."

"Then we'll face them together. They won't kill you, and, if they do, I swear, Night, I will make it my life's mission to put every one of them in the ground."

Not gonna lie, my girl's a goddamn badass. She's so sexy when she turns into this overprotective alpha female.

"I love you, Bethany. You know that, right?"

She nods. "I know, Night, and I love you, too, with every breath in my body. I love you and our son. I always have."

Pulling her to my chest, I place my lips on her forehead, pressing a kiss there and smelling her hair. It brings me comfort, enough so my shakes subside and my head clears a bit more. I have to do this; there's no other option. She's right, and if my brothers can't understand it, so be it. That's a cross I'll bear if I have to.

I'll do anything for my family, for my daydream.

CHAPTER 25

I broke my rules for you.

-Love Quotes

Surprisingly, Twist doesn't try to kill me, as I was expecting. Neither do my brothers. I had forgotten something very important about Twist, that his little girl and first wife were murdered. So he understands why I had to tell his secret. He's prepared to help. Sadie's terrified, but I think she knows Twist is way too psycho to let anything happen to her or their son, Cyle.

Everything goes down according to plan. I get a hair sample from Cyle with Twist's blessing. I drop it off at the store with Sonya like Puppet instructed and then we wait.

I don't know how Puppet pulls it off, but he has results within twenty-four hours. I shouldn't be surprised; the man has obviously been around awhile and wants to know if this boy is part of his family. I was ignorant to think the Iron Fists were stupid. You don't get a reputation like they have by being total dumbasses. It's the last time I underestimate anyone—ever.

The time comes for us to actually meet up. I'm a wreck inside. We've thought about the absolute best ways to go about everything. We've even argued with Puppet over where to meet. Eventually, we come to an agreement, and my woman is vibrating, she's so wound up. Can't say I blame her; I think we all are. Not only does this involve Mav, but there's a chance people will die today.

Bethany follows me in her car, Twist and Cyle ride behind in 2 Piece's truck, and a swarm of our brothers follow behind them. We've agreed that the brothers will stay back, along with Puppet's club. They are here to escort us to and from the meeting point and be ready to come in if it goes south and we need them.

The meeting point is at a scenic overlook on top of a mountain. There aren't many in this area of Texas, and we happen to know the State Troopers travel this route frequently if we need them. We got lucky with Ares' old Prez being in good with the Troopers. They weren't dirty-dirty, but they looked the other way a lot for our club. This is a time we may need to have some law on our side.

Yes we do some bad shit, but we also help make their job easier by cleaning up the filth around the city for them. In return, some things slide under the table, "unnoticed."

Pulling off the side of the road into the gravel, I park. Putting my kickstand down, I glance back to watch Bethany stop and then Twist pull in behind her. The brothers idle near us, waiting.

There's a decent chance this whole thing could go to shit. I hope not 'cause there's two little boys stuck right in the middle of it. I feel like a fucking failure dragging another kid in it, but shit happens. I have to grit through it and do what I have to.

A line of bikes appear from the opposite direction, a truck smack in the middle of the formation. I'm pretty sure we're all in shock. We were expecting their club to be some floaters, maybe some new recruits.

It's fucking huge; I'm talking a good twenty-five rolling up. With what we've discovered about them, too, I doubt this is barely a decent sized chunk of the club. I wouldn't be surprised if the club is a hundred deep or more after seeing them roll up like this. I fucking hate this. Why couldn't it just be a few hellions that I could easily take out. Instead it has to basically be a mob of men for me to work through to get to the middle.

"Motherfucker," I mumble to myself. They could easily shoot us all down if they wanted to; our ten to their twenty-five, no good. I'm glad I told B to stay the fuck in her car or they could take her too.

Sonofabitch. I can't stand feeling as if I'm unprepared, and, in this, it's exactly how I feel. This jackoff has the upper hand besides our wild card being Twist's son.

The motorcycles pull off opposite us, staring us down as the truck pulls to a stop directly in front of me. I make out an older man driving, a little dark head in the middle, and another beefy guy about my size in the passenger seat. If they hurt one hair on Mav's head, you won't be able to peel me off them, I swear.

The older guy says something to the passenger, his gaze flicking over all of us. He gets out, slamming the truck door and I take in the man who's caused so much grief for me. I want to slit his throat so badly that my hands begin to shake. Toeing my kickstand in place, I throw my leg over and come to my full six foot four inches towering over him standing before me.

He doesn't show me any sign that I intimidate him in the slightest which says a lot about his balls right there. I make many men shit bricks, and this one doesn't even blink.

"My son?" I immediately demand, not about to fuck around.

"My grandson?" he counters, and I grit my back teeth together.

"So you believe me now?"

"I told you, I got the DNA results back. I still want to see his face and see if he looks like my boy."

"You bring my son over here, and I'll have Twist show you Cyle."

"I could just kill you and take them hostage you know. We have you out numbered times three."

"Yep, you could. Maybe you haven't heard 'bout Twist though? He'll kill your grandson before he lets you take him. You want any chance of knowing that kid—your blood—you follow through with our agreement."

"Ya know, I like to do whatever the fuck I want usually, but something tells me, you're not fuckin' with me."

I shake my head, glowering down at his five foot-eleven frame, thinking of ten different ways I could kill him right now with my two hands. I'd enjoy every crunch of breaking bone, too.

"Fine," Puppet huffs. "You fuck me over, and my brother," he nods across the street, and I glance, seeing a guy pointing a gun toward my woman's car, "shoots your ol' lady."

"I'm not fucking you over. If he shoots my girl, mark my words, I will slit every motherfucker's throat wearing the Fist's cut."

He grins, showing me a mouth of chipped teeth. He's definitely a hard fucker and has seen a lot. I wouldn't want to be in a club run by him; that, I'm certain of.

Puppet lets out a sharp whistle then meets my gaze as the passenger gets out. I'm able to breathe when I see the big guy grin at Mav and hold his arms out to him. Maverick jumps in his arms and smiles. This tells me that whoever this big fucker is, no matter how much I want to filet him, he was good to my kid.

"Daddy?" Maverick yells and starts waving.

"Hey buddy," I say and hear the car door behind me slam. Bethany comes running to my side.

"Maverick!" she yells, choked up at finally seeing him.

"Mommy!" Our son smiles widely and keeps waving.

The guy carrying him, comes near. I see his name patch says *Viper.*

"My grandson." Puppet holds his hand out, so Viper stalls.

Twisting my head toward Twist, I give him the signal, and he gets out of the truck, Cyle walking beside him like a little badass. With Twist as a father, that kid will no doubt grow up fearless.

Twist stops beside me and flicks his gaze to Puppet. "You fuck with my kid, I slit your fuckin' throat. Got me, pops?"

Puppet flicks his tongue against his teeth and drops his hand. Viper gives Mav a high five and sets him down. Once his feet touch the gravel he's running for Bethany.

"Mommy!" he shouts happily, and my throat grows tight when I see him back in her arms where he belongs. She scoops him up and takes him to her car quickly, not skipping a beat. This is what we planned, and she's followed along perfectly so far.

Puppet asks a few questions, staring at Cyle in a near trance. I tune them out, though. My son is safe. I kept my promise I made to Bethany, and we got our boy back.

"One day, he'll join his family," Puppet states, and Twist rolls his eyes.

"Yeah, okay, old man. He may be your blood, but he's my kid. He carries my name, and I'll continue to raise him. Your blood is part Oath Keeper whether you like it or not. He's a club brat, an Oath Keeper brat."

Puppet hisses, but bites his tongue.

"Where's your President?" he asks me next, still gazing at Cyle.

I turn and gesture to Viking. He rides over, parking next to me.

"Brother." He nods to me.

"Brother," I reply, then gesture to the piece of shit in front of me. "This is Puppet, President of the Iron Fists."

Viking nods, glaring down at the shorter man. "Can I help you?"

"Before I'd have replied, yes, by killing yourself. But I see circumstances have changed."

"You've got guts speaking to me like that, Fist. I'm sure you know who the fuck I am," Viking growls and Puppet smirks.

"I've heard. That being said, I see my grandson is being raised and protected by the Oath Keepers."

Viking nods again.

"Instead of exterminating you, this is grounds for peace from my club."

"We will take the peace, but that does not mean you are welcome in our territory."

"Fine, same goes for your club."

Viking nods again, being his normal solemn self. I wonder what he's really thinking right now. I know we'll take the peace, but once everyone's safe and we're back on our feet, we'll be hunting again. I will kill this motherfucker if it's the last thing I do.

"Twist, you take good care of my grandson. And you ever find yourself in a bind and it has to do with my grandson, you have my help. Otherwise, you better pray you don't die, 'cause if you do, I'm coming for him."

"You fucking wish. I'm going to outlive every fucking cunt here," Twist grits out and spits. He needs to just nod and keep quiet; I'm trying to get us the fuck out of here without any bullets flying.

Viking holds his hand out, and Puppet shakes it. I think both sides let a breath out when they see it. "I'll be in touch," Puppet states, then gestures to Viper, both of them heading back to the truck.

"You okay, brother?" Viking asks out the side of his mouth, keeping his stare trained on the two retreating forms.

"I will be once we're back at the club, and I have them both in my arms."

"You and B take off; we'll follow to make sure you're safe. You, too, Twist; your brothers are at our clubhouse waiting for you."

"Bet," he replies and I crank my engine, waving for Bethany to pull out. I cannot fucking wait to get home with my family.

CHAPTER 26

**You know you're in love when
you can't fall asleep because reality
is finally better than your dreams.**

-Dr. Seuss

I watch my daydream as she giggles with Princess and London. It's been a month since she and I got Maverick back home safely. None of us were expecting to reach peace that day. I believed that we would've ended up in a bloodbath, and I'd have been lucky if B and Mav made it out alive. I'd do anything for them—even pretend to be at peace with a rival club.

Thankfully, the bloodbath didn't happen. I don't know who was watching over us during the exchange, if

He finally heard my plea when I'd hit rock bottom, but something saved us all. It hasn't made me religious in any stretch, but it's made me thankful. I've put things that actually matter in perspective, like my love for Bethany and Maverick along with their happiness.

Her laugh is loud, her smile big, and it makes me feel warm in my chest as the three of them gossip about something. Bethany's grown more beautiful to me the better I've gotten to know her. I haven't touched her like that night we made love though. It was the same night we came up with our plan, and I have to make sure she's one hundred percent ready to go there with me. I have to know she's in love with me as much as I am with her. I would give it all up for her, my club, my life, and my heart.

It may be fucking with me a little bit, too, not touching her. I find myself staring at her all the damn time, to the point my brothers comment on it. She hasn't been back to work either. I barely let her out of my sight. I can't. I know a potential threat is out there, no matter what Puppet says. I won't let harm come to them again.

I need to make her mine. I know inside that she's already mine, but it has to be official. She needs to become my ol' lady in the eyes of the club so I know she has their protection as well. I'll be able to relax more knowing that if something happens to me that they'll look after her and Mav.

"I'm going to do it." I turn to Exterminator, and his eyebrow shoots up.

"No shit?"

Nodding, I repeat myself. "No shit, I'm going to do it." I don't want to wait longer, to hold myself back. I love her too much.

"Good for you, brother." He claps me on my shoulder as Chaos comes to stand next to us.

"'Sup?" he mumbles, tipping his longneck up.

"He's finally gonna do it," Ex grumbles.

"No shit?" Chaos murmurs, and I roll my eyes. These fuckers.

"Jesus, yes, I'm doin' it."

"When?" Viking asks from my left.

Meeting his gaze, there's a challenge shining in it. He doesn't think I'll buck up and actually do it. Taking a deep breath, I admit, "Tonight."

He whistles, and I huff, taking off toward Blaze for another beer. He's chilling, propped up against the counter, finally healed up enough to tend bar. He has to be careful and not move too fast, but he's here. That's what matters, too. We've lost enough brothers over the years. Thankfully, he fought through his injures and came out swinging in the end. If it wasn't for the doc and 2 Piece rushing over to get him to the hospital in time, he'd have died.

"They giving you shit?"

"Yeah, what's new though?"

"What about now?"

"I'm gonna do it." I nod toward Bethany, and Blaze's eyes widen.

"No shit?"

"Oh, for fuck's sake," I grumble throwing my hands up and head straight for her. She's standing at the other end of the bar. These fuckers are going to have me do it right now, just to prove that I'm serious. And I am; I'll do it.

Her gaze hits mine, amused. "Well, looks like someone needs a nap and possibly a spanking." She chortles and the women to her sides giggle. She's gotten ballsier as the days pass, too, and, if I'm honest with myself, I love every damn minute of it.

I've been known to be a bit grouchy around here, and she has me grinning or chuckling like a fool at times. I haven't forgotten what she's done as far as keeping my son from me for all that time, but I've learned to move past it. I'll never forget her actions, but I've forgiven her.

Life is too short and way too precious to fight over shit that's taken up the past. I have a chance to make her and Maverick my future, and I have every intention to do so.

"Aw, baby, someone take your popsicle?" She giggles next, her eyes joyful, knowing she's going to stir me up. Usually I'll just throw her over my shoulder and make her scream when she's in front of her friends like this, but she's in for a surprise today.

"That mouth, Bethany. I swear it'll have my cock in it."

"Oh, he's going to play today." She grins and winks at Princess and I growl. It's a good growl, though. She's making it hard for me to stay serious right now, but I have to.

This won't be real if I don't mean it.

Stepping in front of her, I tower over her as if she's my prey. B's mouth snaps shut when she figures out I'm not going to crack. My fingers go to her face, holding her chin tightly until she can't move away. I can see the heat in them. She can goof off all she wants to, but I know what she wants.

At my touch, she gasps, drawing in a silent breath and my thigh shoots between her legs, parting them for me to squeeze in close. Her back hits the bar and my cock rests against her center, her cheeks tinting at the delicious contact.

Blaze watches from behind the bar wearing a smirk, and I give him a nod. Reaching over, he grips each of her biceps in his palms, securing her in place. She's going nowhere with the hold he has.

Her chest moves quicker as her breaths pick up. My Daydream's getting nervous, thinking that mouth has finally gotten her in the trouble I keep promising. It has, and I couldn't be more excited over it.

I've waited too long for her. She's mine now, and Bethany's about to learn that firsthand right in the middle of the clubhouse bar.

"No more fucking around, you belong to me, Daydream," I promise, my mouth trailing over her neck, teeth grazing her smooth skin until goose bumps appear.

There's no question, no option given, it is what it is, and I'm declaring that shit, no argument permitted. She gets hot when I speak to her like this, and I have to admit it's no problem for me. She wants me to boss her ass and take control in times like these and it's my pleasure.

I slide her hair off to one side, clearing my path and bite into her flesh. I know she loves it. I remember everything she's enjoyed when we've been together. Later I'll have her ride me and I'll pull her hair back while I suck all over her neck, marking her. Everyone will know she's been claimed. They all know she's mine, but she's about to know it and really feel it.

"I do?" she mumbles and I breathe her in. She smells divine like sweet flowers, her usual scent. Everywhere I go, flowers will forever remind me of her, of this moment.

I push the thin material of her slutty red dress up that I know she wore specifically to tease me with. My fingers find her slit, finding her already excited. Bethany's teeth sink into her bottom lip and she's never looked sexier to me. Innocent but oh-so-completely bad. She's just the right mix of crazy to keep me and lock me down as hers forever.

"So fucking wet, too." I slide my digits up and down, readying her for me. "You want me to fuck you right here, right now. Admit it, dollface, you like being fucked where everyone can see us, don't you?" My woman loves filthy talk, gets her even more worked up. My fingers find her clit, rubbing circles, playing with the sensitive bud as she fights to keep quiet and not draw more attention to us.

A moan escapes her as two of my fingers push into her warmth. "Yes," she admits nodding, and I drive them in deeper, rewarding her. Moving them fast, her mouth parts making her pant as I add a third. They pump in and out, stretching her tightness, readying her for my length.

I hurt her our first time when she made me fuck her roughly outside the bar. I wanna be able to fuck her like that again. This time, however, I want her to enjoy every second with no pain from my size.

"No panties either, you bad, bad girl. You must've known I was gonna fuck this pussy tonight," I growl, using my free hand to unbutton my jeans and lower my zipper. This is happening right here, right now, in front of everyone.

Pulling my cock free, I pump the long length a few times, not being able to stop myself. I'm too wound up for her, so damn hard that my dick aches. I want to ram my cock in her and break her in half. Precum tops the head as I imagine bending her over and sinking into her savagely.

The brothers begin wolf-whistling and a few cheer as they see what's going down, finally realizing that I'm one hundred percent serious about claiming her as my property.

"Shit," I hear Viking say from behind me. "Maybe we should make this a club tradition. You want to claim your bitch, you do it in front of all the brothers."

Not surprisingly they hoot and holler, agreeing. Next he's muttering about needing to lick and fuck Princess. I tune them all out as I concentrate on the striking woman in front of me. She's more than ready and more than I could have ever imagined.

Her pussy trembles around my fingers, growing wetter by the moment so I pull them free. "I want your cunt sucking on my cock like that," I groan and line myself up to her entrance. Pushing inside her wet heat, I reach around and press my soaked fingers into her ass at the same time, making her scream out in ecstasy. She never was able to be a quiet one. I guess everyone will know that now as well.

"Mmm," I growl against her throat. "So goddamn tight. This pussy's all mine, you hear? I catch any motherfucker sniffin' around what's mine, and I'll slit their motherfuckin' throat. You understand me, baby?"

"Oh my God," she moans loudly. "Yes, God yes!" she responds, pressing her chest out to brush against my own as I pound into her. Her back is going to be sore as fuck tomorrow, but this will be something that she never forgets; I'll make sure of it. Every time she glances at this bar top, she'll think of me and this moment.

Glancing around briefly, I state loudly, "Mine, you hear? This bitch is all *mine*. My property."

Her pussy drips around my cock, her juices running down my nut sack witnessing me practically beat on my damn chest like a caveman. It's one of the sexiest things coming from a woman that you adore, knowing you have her that turned on. And the fact that it's because I'm claiming her, makes me fall for her even more. I didn't think it's possible, but she easily consumes every single inch of my heart. She loves me with everything, and I love her even more. What else could I ever ask for from my mate?

Her legs clamp around my waist as I drive into her, my fingers matching the rhythm, pressing into her ass again and again. I've had that ass before, and I plan to be there plenty more times, probably starting later tonight. I'm going to sample it all, those plump tits, that ass, and this pussy all over again. I'm going to make her body feel like it's floating on a motherfuckin' cloud, worship her like I would've these past years we've missed.

Minutes pass us, my mind and body lost in complete bliss. "I'm going to fill you up with my cum, then I'm going to eat this pussy until your legs shake," I threaten, yanking her to me with force as my cock explodes inside her with my release. I'm no longer able to hold back, my control completely demolished. She feels too good; I'm too enraptured by her to suppress myself.

After every last drop is free from my now overly-satisfied cock, I lift her off me, her ass landing on the edge of the bar top. My cum dribbles out of her slit making me groan with pure lust. Bethany's like no other woman before. She sets the standard to an entirely new level. I want to lick her from head to toe, nip her skin from top to bottom, and love her like the queen she truly is.

"Give me stars, baby."

She leans back against Blaze's chest as I dive between her thighs, lapping every drop up. I lick and nibble and bite on her until her orgasms peaks and she breaks, coming in front of myself and my brothers with a loud moan.

She sounds beautiful. Knowing I've done that to her, made her feel completely lost and enraptured has me standing a foot taller it seems.

Bringing my forehead to hers, she whispers the sweetest words. "You give me stars, Nightmare. You give me good dreams and you give me love. You can have me. I'm yours, forever."

"Christ, woman."

"I love you, Night."

"I love you, Day," I mutter against her mouth, kissing her passionately with her delicious taste coating my tongue.

It's true, I love her with everything I am, and she's truly the light to my dark, the day to my night, the dreams I've always wanted but have never had.

CHAPTER 27

She knew she loved him when
'home' went from being a
place to being a person.
-E. Leventhal

BETHANY

"I know it's been a few months now and things have been quiet, but do you think we'll ever get to kill Puppet for what he did to Maverick?" I stare at Nightmare, curious.

Since making me his ol' lady last month, he's been pretty open with me when I ask him things about the club. Sure, some things he keeps to himself, but it's usually just the business stuff. I don't need to or want to know about any of that anyhow.

"Trust me, B; I will always have a target on that motherfucker's head. Twist is keeping him alive right now because of Cyle. He doesn't want to have any retaliation harm his family, which I get. But mark my words, dollface, if we ever have the chance, that fucker will be dead before he can blink."

I smile. It's a bit twisted I know, but I have a rage festering so crazy inside to kill the man who stole my son from me, it's insane. I'm not a hateful person, I've always been more peaceful, and the can't-everyone-get-along type.

Something inside you changes when you're a mother and your flesh and blood gets stolen from you. I was beaten and Maverick was forcibly removed from my hands. I'll never forget that experience or the terror he had in his brown irises as they carried him away from me.

Nightmare rarely lets us out of his sight unless he has to go away on business. I know he'll do everything in his power to always keep us safe. He got me a new switchblade, too, and I always carry that sucker everywhere I go. He's taught me how to shoot a gun, and, with practice, I'm getting better.

It all sounds so violent and scary, but it's not. He's teaching me how to protect and defend my family; for that I will forever be grateful to him. I hope I never have to use any of the skills he's taught me, unless the day comes where I can teach Puppet a lesson.

"I hate knowing he's out there," I admit, and his eyes grow distant. He feels the same way. I can sense that in him—the feeling of unfinished business.

"I have a suspicion we'll be seeing more of the Iron Fists in the future. They're like roaches, coming up through the cracks. Besides, Spider won't stop looking for any information we can get on them. We ever lock down a confirmed location and have a way, we will kill them. This, I promise you, dollface."

Shuddering, I wrap my arms around his waist and lean my head against his chest. "I love you, Night. I don't think I ever said the words when we got Maverick, but thank you for getting our son back."

"Daydream, I'll fight until my last breath to keep you both safe—always

"I know. We're lucky to have you."

"Nah, baby, it's me who's the lucky one. I love you, too, Bethany."

"So, what's the plan now?"

"Well, the floors have been replaced. I even repainted the living room and hall at the house, so you guys can finally come home. I can't believe it's taken so long. I just had to make sure it was safe first."

"I know. So we'll be okay then?"

"Yeah, I also had Spider hook up some security features. We have some cameras and an automatic door lock. It locks as soon as the door closes on its own and you can only enter by using your thumbprint, so no jimmying the lock or getting a spare key to break in. I put the chain on the inside too, so no explorer Mav getting out."

"Wow, that sounds high tech."

"It is, but I have to know you're protected when I'm not at home."

"And here I thought you liked keeping us at the clubhouse."

"I do, but too much shit goes on around here, I don't want Maverick seeing it. Plus, I'm afraid one day Honey will piss you off enough that she'll go to sleep and never wake up again. I did get you that new switchblade, and I know a few brothers whose dicks would be sad if that happened."

"As long as none of those dicks belong to you, then I'll let her keep breathing." I wink and he chuckles.

"You're such a badass, babe." He grins and places a tender kiss to my forehead.

"Only for you guys. I'm just protecting what's mine," I mumble into his shirt and he squeezes me to him more.

"Exactly, I'm yours." He kisses me again, and I feel his breath in my hair. He's always smelling it and sighing. I've kept the same shampoo just for that reason. "Now, we ready for this late birthday party? There's a three year old who deserves to get spoiled by his family."

"Definitely, I can't wait to see him surprised."

"As long as he likes a motorcycle cake, then we're good."

"He will absolutely love it; he's just like his dad." I smile and kiss his cheek.

If I could go back in time, would I do things different? I'd like to say no, but that'd be a lie.

Nightmare deserved to be a father from the very beginning, and I took that away from him.

I plan to spend the rest of my life showing him just how much I love him and give him the chance to be a father. Who knows, maybe down the road we'll have another. Right now, though, I'm being selfish and only sharing him with Maverick.

Time's so easily lost; we need to learn to spend it with the ones we love, doing the things we love. In the end, the small things will be the big things. I'm just grateful to have learned that now before it was too late and more time was wasted.

I'll never get those years back, but I'll love Nightmare every single day for the rest of my life. He is, after all, the one who made me see stars.

Sapphire Knight

EPILOGUE

**There are two gifts we should
give our children; one is roots,
and the other is wings.**

- Unknown

MAVERICK

13 years later...

"Ummm...what do you mean I can't have a motorcycle? I'm sixteen, Mom, and it's my birthday."

"Not happening, Mav. You have to wait until you're eighteen, you know this. We've already talked about it." She shakes her head and my dad's gaze hits his boots. He's in a huge pile of shit with her and he knows it. She doesn't though, not yet.

"Uh, Daydream?" he mutters, clearing his throat. It's pretty entertaining, we both dwarf my mom, but she's the boss in the end. She can bring a grown man to his knees. My dad with a simple kiss, anyone else and her switchblade will do the trick. "I, uh, sorta got the kid a bike." He coughs and I snort. He gives me so much shit when I choke up fessing something to my mom.

"You didn't."

"I did." He sighs and I grin at mom.

Interrupting, I pull my leather jacket on. "Yeah, so you two sort this out. I'm taking off."

"And where in the hell do you think you're going exactly?" Her attention snaps to me, pinning me down with steel in her gaze.

My Aunt Princess has the same look when she's serious, too. Thankfully, she thinks I can do no wrong, so it's never turned on me. Mom. though, she'll shoot it at me every time I'm two minutes late coming in the door.

"I need to pick up Jessie."

"Jessie, as in Jessica? Cain and London's daughter?" Her eyes widen.

"Yes, ma'am."

"Oh, Jesus Christ." She stares down my dad next, "I'm so blaming you for this shit." She shakes her head, exasperated and walks off.

314

Daydream

She's too concerned with Jessie's father getting pissed that she's not even thinking of the bike anymore. I've learned how to distract her like Dad does.

He turns to me with a devilish grin. "Go get her, son." We fist bump and I'm out the door.

It's on like Donkey Kong. Hope Jessie knows she's mine, cause if not, she's about to figure it out.

I am, after all, just like my dad, and life's nothing but a daydream.

THE END

THANK YOU...

Thank you for reading Daydream! I really hope you enjoyed Nightmare and Bethany's story. Many of you sent me messages asking me for more from them. I hope this satisfied that craving and has made you excited for the next.

Yes, there will be more; you can never have too many bikers! I'm working on Saint and Sinner next and can't wait to unleash their brand of crazy on you all.

Once again, thank you. Your support means more than you know! If you enjoyed this book, please take a moment to leave a review. It can be short and sweet, every bit helps.

XOXO- Sapphire

STAY UP TO DATE WITH SAPPHIRE

Email

authorsapphireknight@yahoo.com

Website

www.authorsapphireknight.com

Facebook

www.facebook.com/AuthorSapphireKnight

CPSIA information can be obtained
at www.ICGtesting.com
Printed in the USA
LVOW07s1436151017
552521LV00020B/391/P